A Legac

Once again, Detec
Richard Tansey and Detective-Sergeant Bill Abbot of the Thames Valley Police are in familiar territory, this time investigating mysterious events at a coeducational day and boarding-school near Colombury in the Cotswolds. A sixteen-year-old girl, Hannah Aston, is facing a desperate dilemma which results in her disappearance on the night of the school's Hallowe'en Party, spirited away like one of the supernatural beings whose costumed embodiments throng the assembly hall. But the mystery of the girl's disappearance is not as inexplicable as at first appears. A surprising number of people turn out to know something about Hannah and her problems.

There is a legacy, of course—a legacy of death—and it is a legacy which leads Tansey and Abbot into a wilderness of contradictory evidence and misleading red herrings. It is only after a dramatic climax that all becomes unambiguous.

by the same author

DEATH'S LONG SHADOW
A KNIFE ILL-USED
A FEAST OF DEATH
OUTRAGEOUS EXPOSURES
ACCIDENT PRONE
BARREN REVENGE
UNTO THE GRAVE
A DEADLY SICKNESS
MORTAL TERM
A WILL TO KILL
DECEITFUL DEATH
NOTICE OF DEATH

JOHN PENN

A Legacy of Death

THE CRIME CLUB
An Imprint of HarperCollins *Publishers*

First published in Great Britain in 1992
by The Crime Club, an imprint of
HarperCollins Publishers, 77–85 Fulham Palace Road,
Hammersmith, London W6 8JB

9 8 7 6 5 4 3 2 1

John Penn asserts the moral right to be identified
as the author of this work.

A catalogue record for this book is
available from the British Library

ISBN 0 00 232411 3

Photoset in Linotron Baskerville by
Rowland Phototypesetting Ltd
Bury St Edmunds, Suffolk
Printed and bound in Great Britain by
HarperCollins Book Manufacturing, Glasgow

This book is fiction.
Any relationship between the characters in this novel
and any person who exists in reality
is purely coincidental.

CHAPTER 1

The girl lay face down, trying to smother her sobs in a pillow that was already wet with her tears. She had been crying for some while. Her body was hot and sticky. From time to time it shook, as if in a paroxysm of frustration or suppressed anger, leaving her feeling weak. Suddenly, after one such paroxysm, she knelt up on the bed and, regardless of the noise she might be making, punched the pillow again and again with clenched fists.

'I hate him!' she muttered. 'I hate him! How could he do this to me? How could he?'

Then, her spurt of temper spent, she collapsed once more and wept. She wished herself dead. The grandfather clock, one of the family's prized possessions, started to strike, and the girl counted the strokes that resounded from the hall below throughout the small house. She counted to twelve. It was midnight—another day. But nothing had changed. She was pregnant. There was no need for any pregnancy testing kit such as the girls at her last school used to giggle about. She had missed two periods and had even felt a little sick one morning, so there was no doubt in her mind.

At least, she reflected, it was a Saturday and she was under no compulsion to go to school, but she remembered that she was due to have her weekly riding lesson at ten. Of course she could say she was feeling unwell, which was true enough. Or could she? It would mean enduring her mother's silent reproaches. The lessons were expensive, and unless forty-eight hours' notice was given Audrey Driver insisted on payment; one could hardly blame her as the riding school represented the Drivers' livelihood, but still . . .

Eventually Hannah Aston found herself lying on her side in a stupor, her *crise de nerfs* over. It had exhausted her, but had achieved nothing else. She couldn't recall ever having been so unhappy, so desperate.

Hannah was sixteen. She was of medium height and well developed for her age. But what was most noticeable about her was her colouring. Her long straight hair could only be described by a simile; it was like corn with light shining on it, and her eyes, though not large, were an unusual shade of violet. Her other features were undistinguished, except for her thin aquiline nose, which saved her from being merely pretty and gave a promise of real beauty to come.

Tonight, her eyes bloodshot and swollen from weeping, her nose red and her skin blotched, she knew she must look positively ugly. Even her hair was bedraggled. Slowly she turned on to her back, sat up and swung her legs over the side of the bed. She realized that she had to do something about her appearance or she wouldn't be presentable in the morning. She might be able to fend off her mother's questions by pleading a headache, but an excuse like that wouldn't satisfy her friend Marjorie's curiosity or stop Rodney Driver from making embarrassing remarks.

Hannah opened her bedroom door cautiously, and went along the passage to the bathroom as quietly as she could, envying Marjorie, who lived in a much larger house and had her own bathroom. She reached her objective unnoticed, put on the light, and ran the cold water tap. She bathed her face for several minutes and patted some of her mother's astringent lotion on to her skin; it didn't seem to make any difference. She would just have to hope for the best. Perhaps if she could get a few hours' sleep—But how could she sleep when she was so utterly miserable?

Unthinkingly, she worked the flush before starting back

to bed. As usual, her parents' door was ajar, and as she passed it she paused, knowing what to expect.

'Is that you, Hannah dear?'

Hannah was tempted to reply, 'No, Mother, it's a burglar.' Instead she said, 'It's all right, Mother. I needed to go to the lavatory.'

'Very well, dear. Try to sleep now.'

Hannah didn't bother to answer. She marched along to her room and shut the door firmly. She told herself that she would not cry any more. She would be sensible. She was not the first person to whom this had happened, and she wouldn't be the last. Others had got rid of unwanted babies and so would she, though how this was to be done without her mother knowing was a problem. Because her mother must not know. She would nag and nag about who was responsible, until in desperation Hannah would tell her —and the resulting scene would be unimaginable. Poor Mother, Hannah thought, with all her high hopes and ambitions for me.

She gritted her teeth. She must forget her troubles for the moment. Her mother's admonition hadn't been without sense. She must try to sleep.

Disturbed by his wife, Richard Aston also felt the need to go to the bathroom. He hoped that when he returned Irene would be asleep once more, but she was awake, sitting up, with the lamp on her bedside table switched on. After twenty years of marriage he knew what this meant. Irene would want to talk, to mull over whatever she believed to be their current problem. Richard got into bed and resigned himself.

'I'm worried about Hannah, Richard,' Irene began. 'She's not been looking well lately. "Peaky" is what my mother would have called it. Do you think we're putting too much strain on her?'

'Making her work too hard, you mean? Irene, if she doesn't work hard she'll never get a place at Oxford.'

'I realize that, and it's very good of Mr Blondel to give her extra coaching, but she won't be going up till the year after next, and she has so many other interests—the school play, and games and dancing and her clothes and—'

'Riding on Saturday mornings?'

Irene ignored this addition to her list. 'It's cycling to and from school every day that's such an effort for her.'

'Irene, it's only about twenty minutes on a bike, and I drive her when the weather's bad or, if I don't, then Mary Eversley takes her with Marjorie.' Richard smothered a yawn. This was an enduring discussion; he knew where it was going to lead and he resented it. 'After all, it was you who insisted on sending her to Coriston.'

'Of course.' Irene was unrepentant. 'Once the College started to take day pupils it was obvious she should go there. Her old school was a dreadful place. She'd never have got into Oxford from there, and some of the other students—really! Richard, you must realize that it's important she should make nice friends now, friends who will last into later life.'

'Such as Alan Carson?'

'Why not? You and Alan's father were at Sandhurst together. Or would you prefer she went around with Peter Merger?' Irene was tart.

Richard grinned. 'If she did I might get a discount on my wine and spirits bill. Don't forget, my dear, the younger Merger boy—what's his name? Ian, that's it—is at Coriston, and he's a boarder.'

It was the wrong remark for Richard to have made. Although she tried to make light of the matter by saying how much they would miss not having Hannah at home, Irene Aston was bitter that they couldn't afford to send their daughter to Coriston as a boarder. Both Irene and her sister had been to boarding schools, Richard had been at Marlborough, and she was grieved that they couldn't afford to give Hannah all the advantages they had had themselves.

Finally she said, 'Well, we'd better try to sleep. We've a busy day ahead of us.'

She put out her bedside light and snuggled under the bedclothes, turning her back on her husband. Soon she heard his gentle snores and, as always, wondered at his capacity for sleep; he claimed it was a relic of his army days when sometimes it was essential to snatch sleep whenever and wherever it was possible. Slumber did not come so easily to her. She lay awake, hearing the grandfather clock strike one, then two, then three.

Irene Aston was in her mid-forties. Once she had been a pretty girl, blonde, blue-eyed, the younger daughter of a devoted couple, her father a Brigadier, her mother a distant relation of an aristocratic family. Her parents had been killed in a car crash in the late seventies, but by then she was happily married to Richard Aston and had a small daughter. Richard was on his way to a successful career in the army, and their future looked assured.

It hadn't turned out like that. Promotion in the army had been slow and, after defence cuts, Richard had found himself retired with the rank of Major at the age of forty-two. Suddenly, instead of life being simple, everything had become difficult. Used to Service accommodation, they had no home and not a great deal of money with which to buy one, especially as prices had soared to such an extent.After five years in Germany, England seemed strange and unfriendly. Then Richard had become ill with some obscure kind of fever and while he was in hospital in Oxford Irene had bought their present house outside the Cotswold market town of Colombury.

She had intended this to be a temporary arrangement, but once again she was proved wrong. Richard recovered quite quickly, but showed no inclination to move or to get himself paid work of any kind; he had, he said, done his bit. He had a good pension and, even after the house was bought, albeit with a large mortgage, there still remained a little private money. They could live very comfortably, he maintained, either forgetting inflation or choosing to disregard it.

And now, after five years, Irene was resigned. She had a strong sense of duty. But it always infuriated her when Richard ordered drinks all around in a crowded bar of the Windrush Arms. It was money they could ill afford, and would certainly be far better spent on Hannah. Irene no longer cared for herself, but she minded very much about Hannah.

She turned over on to her other side. She must stop worrying about money and Hannah. She needed the sleep. What she had said to Richard was true: they had a busy day ahead.

The Astons' early morning was normally geared to suit Hannah, who had to leave for school at a quarter past eight, but Richard liked to get up early, even at weekends. He was a methodical man. When the alarm beside his bed burred he rose at once, collected his clothes—carefully laid ready the night before—and went to the bathroom to shower and shave and dress. He then went down to the kitchen and made tea. He poured himself a mug, and took a tray up to Irene.

This was, she considered, her one luxury, and she enjoyed it. Richard, accustomed to a batman, was not domesticated and did little to help in the house. But he gardened, grew vegetables with varying degrees of success and ferried Hannah around when necessary. He also worked for the local office of the British Legion, unpaid, and for various other voluntary and charitable organizations, where he was found to be efficient, dependable and pleasant to deal with. He had become a popular figure in Colombury.

This was a particularly busy time of year for him, and indeed for many other people. The most important event was the march to the Colombury war memorial and the service on Remembrance Sunday, but there was also the harvest festival, the church fair, Hallowe'en and the town firework display and bonfire on Guy Fawkes night. To a greater or lesser degree they each involved a certain amount of effort from Richard and, he had to admit, except for the fireworks, for Irene too. But on the whole he enjoyed it.

His tea finished, he swilled out his mug and put it in the plastic draining basket. Soon afterwards Irene came downstairs with her early morning tea-tray, closely followed by Hannah. Irene thought her daughter looked tired and rather unwell, but refrained from commenting. Richard nodded his approval at her slim figure set off by jodhpurs and a scarlet sweater that emphasized the swell of her breasts. He thought with regret that his little girl was fast becoming a woman.

'Scrambled eggs and mushrooms,' Irene said cheerfully, busy at the stove.

'Good,' said Richard, pushing aside his cereal bowl. 'I'm hungry.' He was one of those tall thin men who can eat as much as they like without putting on weight.

'Not for me,' Hannah said. 'Just toast, please.'

'You must eat, darling. Try a little. They're fresh eggs from the farm.' Irene was anxious.

'We don't want you wasting away.'

Hannah ignored her father's flippancy and averted her eyes from the golden mound of eggs and mushrooms that Irene had put in front of him. 'Just toast, please,' she repeated firmly. She was sure that if she ate even a mouthful of the stuff she would be sick.

'Very well,' Irene said, avoiding an argument.

'What are you two doing today?' Hannah asked brightly, eager to change the subject. She was not really interested, but she had interpreted her father's and her mother's quick appraisals, and she had no wish to be forced to reply to further comments. 'What about lunch?' she asked.

Irene was determined that Hannah, as an only child, should not be spoilt. 'You'll have to get your own and your father's for once, when you come back from the Drivers'. There's cold meát and salad in the refrigerator, and you can heat up what's left of the soup from last night's supper.'

'What about you?' Hannah's tone of voice made it clear that she didn't approve of Irene's proposal.

'I shall take sandwiches and have them in the car. Mrs Gorel is ill and I've promised to do her Meals on Wheels round this morning. It's not easy for them to find substitutes on a Saturday. Then I'll be able to go straight on to the church to help prepare for tomorrow's festival.'

'All your good works,' Hannah muttered under her breath, not caring if her mother heard.

Irene opened her mouth to make a sharp retort, but Richard intervened. 'In the circumstances I think I'll go to the pub and have sandwiches there. I'll be at the Legion HQ all day stuffing envelopes for the appeal. November 11th isn't far off now. You'll be all right about getting to the riding school, won't you, Hannah?'

'Yes, Marjorie and her mother are picking me up at about ten to ten.'

Irene suppressed a sigh; she knew that Richard's 'sandwiches at the pub' meant the Windrush Arms and at least a couple of gins. 'Then, if your father's going to be out, you'll have only yourself to look after, Hannah. Don't forget to take the back door key or you won't be able to get into the house. Come along to the church afterwards, if you like, we can do with an extra pair of hands.'

'I can't,' Hannah said. 'I've got to write an essay for Monday—on the causes of the Second World War.'

It was a spontaneous lie and, she realized at once, a stupid one—or at least a stupid choice of subject. Major Aston had been born too late to remember that war. But he had been keen on military history and had learnt a great deal about it from his father. Hannah had no alternative but to listen to a lengthy and boring lecture, largely based on anecdotal evidence, while Irene washed up the breakfast dishes and got ready to leave.

She was thankful when the front door shut behind her parents.

CHAPTER 2

Mrs Eversley picked Hannah up at a quarter to ten. Hannah could easily have cycled to the riding stables, but as Mrs Eversley was driving Marjorie it was no trouble to take Hannah too. Marjorie liked Hannah's company and was glad that they were in the same form at Coriston, and Hannah liked riding in the Eversleys' Jaguar instead of her father's beaten up Ford. In many ways it was a rather unequal friendship.

Each girl envied the other—and with some reason. Marjorie envied Hannah her appearance and her health. Marjorie herself was an excessively thin girl, inclined to illness. She had spindly limbs, narrow shoulders and a long face. One day she might well be a beautiful woman, but now in her teens she was plain and unattractive. She was also shy, a fact she tried to hide by constant nervous chattering. She thought that Hannah was sophisticated and altogether admirable.

Hannah envied Marjorie not for her personal qualities,

but for her lifestyle, which she knew was what her mother would have wished for her. Bill Eversley was a successful solicitor. The Eversleys owned a large stone house with a fine garden, which included a tennis court and a swimming pool. They ran two cars. They went ski-ing in the winter and to Europe or America for their summer holiday. They talked of buying a house in France. They seemed a happy and contented family, especially when Marjorie's elder brothers, both now at Cambridge, were at home.

Hannah, a perceptive girl, had noticed that she was no longer asked to the Eversleys' when the boys were there. There had been an unpleasant incident when, teasing her, they had seized her suddenly and demanded that she kiss them *à la Française*, as they called it, with open mouths. Frightened and angry, she had smacked Harold across the face. They had let her go at once, shocked by her reaction, and had apologized, but they had never forgiven her.

Not that she cared. Friendship with Marjorie suited her, but she could do without the boys. A cousin of Irene Aston's had been at school with Mary Eversley and had effected the introduction when the Astons came to Colombury, but it had remained a casual relationship. The families met frequently because of their daughters and their church and the fact that they lived in a small place. But the adults didn't entertain each other, except at the cocktail party the Eversleys gave every Christmas. The Astons never returned this hospitality.

This morning Marjorie was bubbling with enthusiasm. 'I'm going to the Hallowe'en party as a bat,' she said. 'Mum's given me an old black chiffon evening dress she doesn't like any more, and we're going to adapt it.'

'Sounds great,' Hannah said indifferently.

'What are you wearing this year, Hannah?' asked Mary Eversley, meaning to be kind.

'My witch costume,' Hannah was short. This would be

the third time she had worn it. 'It's not worth much effort for one night.'

'That's what some of the men teachers seem to think,' said Marjorie. 'All they do is put on a dinner jacket, pin a tail on the back, wear a headdress with horns and a fierce mask, and, behold! a fetching devil. I think it shows a lack of imagination.'

Her mother laughed. 'Do many of them do that?'

'A dozen or so, usually. I bet Rod Driver would be more original, if he were a master at Coriston.'

Marjorie, to her mother's amusement, was a little in love with her riding master, which was not altogether surprising. He was an extremely good-looking man in his early thirties with a charismatic but slightly old-fashioned swashbuckling air. Marjorie had no trouble picturing him fighting a duel to protect her honour. Nor was she the only one. The stables flourished half on Rodney's charm and half on Audrey Driver's ability and business acumen. People sometimes speculated about why he should have married a short, dumpy woman several years his senior, but naturally no one dared to inquire. Certainly, they appeared a very happy couple.

'Good morning, ladies.'

Rodney Driver came forward to greet them as the Jaguar drove into the yard. He opened the car doors and made a gesture towards helping Mrs Eversley out. He noted with amusement that, whereas Hannah leapt out of her own accord, Marjorie waited for him to offer her his hand. He was not a stupid man.

'I'll just pop into the office to settle my account,' said Mary Eversley. 'I'll be back as usual to fetch the girls.'

'Splendid. Many thanks.' Rodney gave her a warm smile, which he then transferred to Marjorie and Hannah. 'I planned that this morning we'd go along to the top field and practise a little jumping. Nothing too difficult,' he reassured them. 'I'll get the horses.'

As he left them Marjorie looked anxiously at Hannah. 'Are you all right? You're looking very pale and you hardly said a word in the car.'

'I'm fine.' Hannah was brusque; in fact, after such a miserable night she wasn't feeling too well and was not in the best of tempers.

Marjorie, rebuffed, was silent. Driver returned leading two horses, a roan, a lively animal by the name of Vain Glory, and a grey, an armchair of a horse, called Snowball.

'Can I ride Vain Glory?' Hannah asked at once. 'I rode Snowball last time.'

Rodney Driver hesitated. Of the two girls Marjorie was much the better horsewoman, but that wasn't the only consideration. He had seen the disappointment on Marjorie's face as soon as Hannah spoke, and he needed to keep her good will. He didn't want her complaining to her mother, as Audrey had said she must have done. The Eversleys were good customers and they paid their bills on time—which was more than could be said for the Astons, who had on occasion to be reminded. But Hannah of the lovely hair, as he thought of her . . . In the end, he compromised.

'OK. You start with Glory, Hannah. Then you and Marjorie can swap later.'

'Thanks.'

He gave each girl a leg-up, collected his own horse and, to compensate Marjorie, rode beside her along the track that led from the stables to the field where the jumps were laid out. Hannah followed them, pleased to have got her own way.

At the field they found Audrey Driver with a party of four, a couple of young women whom Hannah hadn't seen before, a small boy on a fat pony, and Alan Carson who was a weekly boarder at Coriston and rode most Saturdays.

Hannah was unaware of the suppressed irritation with which Audrey regarded her as she sat triumphantly on Vain Glory. Meeting Audrey in the town a few days ago, Mary Eversley had said, 'I wish you'd put Marjorie up on your better horses, Audrey. She won't improve if she always rides old hacks. And I wouldn't mind paying a little extra.' But, in spite of her having warned Rod, Audrey thought bitterly, here was the Aston girl on the roan, and Marjorie on old Snowball. She strode over to them.

'All right. Let's not waste time. Get into line and go over the small jumps first. We'll criticize and, I hope, have reason to praise.' Audrey was businesslike.

The lesson began. It wasn't easy to deal with half a dozen pupils with varying degrees of ability, but the Drivers were professionals and they worked well together. After a short interval Rodney Driver peeled off the more experienced of the two young women and Alan Carson, who was by far the most competent horseman of the bunch, and took them across to what were considered the more difficult jumps.

Alan lifted a hand to Hannah and Marjorie in a mock farewell. Marjorie waved in reply. Hannah made no response. Alan was an attractive young man, very fair and rather effeminate in facial appearance, but he disliked being ignored and, as he watched Hannah, his grey eyes were cold.

'What I want you to do next,' Audrey was saying,' is each in turn to walk your horse quietly up to the water jump so that he can have a good look at it. Then come back and go for it at a gallop.' She regarded Hannah speculatively, wondering if she might suggest that she should change horses with Marjorie. 'Hannah—'

'Right,' Hannah said immediately, guessing Audrey's intention. She did not want to relinquish Glory for old Snowball, and Mrs Driver had been picking on her, criticizing her throughout the lesson. She would show her she could ride.

Hannah led Vain Glory to the water jump, turned, trotted back, then set off at a gallop. Normally Glory was quite capable of clearing the jump with ease, but this morning the horse was lazy and bored. He sensed that his rider was inexperienced. He landed with two feet in the water and splashed through.

This infuriated Hannah. Already in a black mood, she lost her temper. She hit the horse hard with her whip, harder than she had intended and, foolishly, instead of on the rump, across Vain Glory's head. The result was disastrous. The horse suddenly veered to the right, made for the hedge between the field and a lane and took a huge leap over it, throwing Hannah into the ditch.

For the Drivers this was a crisis and a potential calamity. Hannah, for whom they were responsible, had managed to crawl out of the ditch and now lay on the grass verge, breathing heavily. Vain Glory, satisfied with what he had achieved, was trotting down the lane, to be caught by Audrey, who saw at once that he had a cut on his left hind leg and was lame; he would be out of action for several days at least.

Cursing, she turned her attention to Hannah. Rodney had already reached the girl and was bending over her. He had had the presence of mind to shout to Alan Carson to take charge of the other horses and riders. Vain Glory would have to wait. Hannah, Audrey knew, had to be their main concern.

As Audrey arrived she saw Hannah push Rodney away, and heard her scream, 'Don't touch me, damn you! Don't touch me.' Rodney sat back on his heels, looked up at his wife and shook his head. He mimed puzzlement.

Audrey also knelt on the grass beside Hannah. Naturally, as riding instructors, she and Rodney had seen many falls and had some knowledge of first aid. 'How are you?' she said gently. 'That was a nasty fall.' But Hannah was already getting to her feet, and Audrey put out an arm to steady her. 'Thank goodness, you don't seem to have broken anything. Do you hurt anywhere in particular?'

'No. I'm all right,' Hannah said, and started to cry.

Audrey took the girl's face in her hands and looked into her eyes. 'No concussion as far as I can tell,' she said to her husband. 'The tears are just shock. What do you think—a doctor?'

Rodney shook his head.

'You're sure you don't hurt anywhere, Hannah? You don't feel sick or dizzy or anything?' Audrey persisted.

'I'm all right, I tell you,' said Hannah,

She was angry at what had happened. She knew the story would be all round Coriston on Monday, thanks to Alan Carson, and she would have to endure some unfunny jokes at her expense.

Audrey hesitated. 'I think the best thing would be for me to drive you home,' she said. Luckily I brought the car up here and didn't ride.' She gave Hannah a handkerchief and started to dust her down. 'Rod, you go back to the others, and take Vain Glory—I'll send Stan to collect him.' Stan was the lad at the stables. 'We may need the vet, but let's hope not.'

'Right. See you later.' He grinned at Hannah. 'Cheer up, sweetie. Everyone gets thrown from a horse sooner or later.'

Hannah did not respond. She continued to cry as Audrey helped her along the lane to the car. In spite of what she had told Audrey, her ankle hurt and she had bruised her right hip, but those minor injuries didn't account for the tears which she seemed unable to control. It wasn't until she was almost home that she managed to regain her composure.

'I'm sorry about Vain Glory,' she said. 'He's not badly hurt, is he?'

'He's got a nasty cut on one of his hind legs. There must have been something sharp in the ditch. Providing it wasn't rusty he'll be all right.' Audrey hesitated again. 'Hannah, I don't understand. How did it happen? Glory's used to the water jump and he's never—panicked before.'

'I don't know. I can't remember.' This was Hannah's story and she intended to stick to it.

Audrey sighed. 'Well, I'd better come in and explain to your mother.'

'She's not home. She's doing a "Meals on Wheels" round, and Dad's at the British Legion. I'll phone him there and I expect he'll come. But there's no need for you to wait. I'm fine. Nothing to worry about.' Hannah was scrambling out of the car almost before it had come to a halt.

'Many thanks for bringing me home,' she said. 'Apologies for Glory and for all my tears. Stupid of me. As you said, it was the shock.'

Hannah gave Audrey a brilliant smile and ran. Her one desire was to be alone. Somehow the accident had been the last straw. She slammed the back door shut behind her, leant against it and relaxed. She closed her eyes, then opened them at once as she pictured Rodney Driver's face bending close to hers as if he were about to kiss her. Whatever her mother said, she vowed she was not going to the Drivers' riding school again. She didn't enjoy riding, and it was a waste of time and money—merely one of her mother's snob ideas.

She went into the sitting-room and looked out of the window. Audrey was still there, a small square figure behind the steering-wheel. Hannah waited. She prayed that Audrey, from some mistaken sense of guilt, would not change her mind and decide that she couldn't be left by herself, and she breathed a sigh of relief when at last the car drove off. Now at least she could be alone with her misery. She had no intention of asking her father to come.

Mrs Aston phoned the Drivers that evening. She made no effort to be pleasant. She said that Hannah was bruised and badly shaken. It was a mercy she was no worse; she could have broken a limb, or been concussed. She might even have been killed. Surely they might have sent for a doctor, either at the scene or before leaving the girl alone in an empty house. However, what was done was done, but in the circumstances Mrs Driver would understand that Hannah would not be continuing her lessons at the riding school.

Audrey didn't attempt to explain. She merely said yes, she did understand, and she would be sending Mrs Aston her account to date. She was white with anger as she banged down the receiver. It was true that she had had doubts about leaving Hannah alone, but Hannah, who after all wasn't exactly a child, had been insistent that she would be all right until her father came—and there had been the riding school to consider, the next lot of pupils, Glory's injury. Mrs Aston had no justification for speaking to her in such a peremptory manner

'I've a damned good mind to send Lady High and Mighty the vet's bill too,' she said to her husband. 'God knows what old Meredith will charge for coming out here in his lunch hour and giving Glory a couple of injections.'

'Stan thought it was a good idea to have him looked at as soon as possible. The cut showed signs of rust around the edges and we don't want to lose Glory. We'll have to do without him for a week as it is, which will be nuisance enough.' Rodney sounded depressed. 'I'm sorry, darling. It's my fault. I ought never to have let the wretched girl ride Vain Glory.'

'I don't understand it. What did she do to the horse to panic him like that?'

'I wouldn't swear to it, but when I went back into the field Alan Carson said, "Stupid little bitch, she hit Glory across the head. No wonder he bolted. And of course she had no idea how to control him." You know, Audrey, Alan could be a useful witness if the Astons decided to make trouble.'

'Yes.' Audrey didn't trust Alan Carson completely. 'I thought he and Hannah were pretty friendly.'

Rodney shrugged. 'I'd say he had more in common with Marjorie, though I doubt if he fancies either of them. Anyway, if any nasty rumours start spreading around the place we'll have some support to counteract them.'

'And what did Marjorie say?'

'She agreed with Alan. At least she didn't contradict him.'

'That's a blessing. The last thing we want is to lose the Eversleys' business.' Audrey smothered a yawn. 'Let's go to bed, Rod. It's been a horrid day. Accidents don't do riding schools any good at all.'

'Indeed not.' Rodney stood up and stretched. 'Damn the little bitch!' he said.

CHAPTER 3

Irene Aston checked over the items on Hannah's breakfast tray. Hannah had asked for coffee, orange juice, muesli and toast. Irene had added a boiled egg; she was sure Hannah was not eating enough. The tray was heavy, and she carried it slowly up the stairs and along the passage to Hannah's room. She had insisted that, after the previous day's accident which could so easily have been serious, Hannah should sleep late and have breakfast in bed.

She found Hannah sitting up against a pile of pillows

and reading or pretending to read. In fact, Hannah had been planning what she would do the next day, Monday. It was ironic, she thought, that the bad fall from Vain Glory which could so easily have been a Godsend and caused her to have a miscarriage had had no effect whatsoever. If she had wanted the damned baby, she would have lost it for sure. As it was, at least it had given her an idea. There was a time-honoured remedy that might be worth trying. It probably wouldn't work, but—

'Here's your breakfast, dear,' said Irene.

'Oh Mum, thank you, but you needn't have,' Hannah said as Irene settled the tray on her lap. 'I could easily have come down as usual.'

'It doesn't hurt to have a treat occasionally, and after yesterday . . . ' Irene left the sentence unfinished. 'I can't understand that Driver woman leaving you alone in the house as she did. You'd think she'd have felt some responsibility.'

'I was all right.'

'But you might not have been. Now, tell me, how are you feeling this morning?'

'Fine!' This was not completely true. Hannah's bruises were painful and her ankle was slightly swollen. But she didn't want to talk about her health. 'Don't fuss, Mum. Please.'

'Are you sure you wouldn't like to stay in bed and give church a miss today?'

'Perfectly sure, Mum. I always enjoy Harvest Festival, and if I don't go people will start asking questions. I'm certain Marjorie will have spread the glad tidings of my little contretemps yesterday and—'

'Is that all you call it—a little contretemps?'

'I know. It could have been nasty, but it wasn't, and I want to forget about it. I don't want a fuss.'

'All right, dear. I understand.' Irene bent and kissed

Hannah. 'I'm so thankful there was no great damage done. Have your breakfast and come down when you like. We'll be leaving for church around a quarter to eleven, as usual.'

'OK. Thanks again, Mum.'

Hannah smiled at Irene with real affection. The idea that her mother 'understood' was ludicrous, a black joke. But it didn't matter. She didn't understand her mother either. Irene's ambitions for her daughter, her 'good works', her snobbishness and the great efforts she made to cook and clean and keep the house as she thought it should be kept, were a mystery to Hannah. Nevertheless, she loved her mother dearly, reluctantly admired her, yet pitied her; but she wouldn't have dreamt of confiding in her.

Hannah propped the book she had been pretending to read—a novel that Stephen Blondel, her form master, who also taught her English, had recommended—against the coffee pot and started to eat her breakfast. To please her mother she ate the egg. In spite of her aches and pains she was feeling more hopeful today.

'Not the best of Harvest Festivals!' said Irene Aston as they drove home.

'The church was beautiful,' Richard said. 'I particularly liked that huge sheaf of corn in the corner behind the font.'

Irene snorted. 'That was Mrs Merger's bright idea. But what use is a sheaf of corn? The fruit and vegetables and flowers can go to the hospital or the poor tomorrow, but corn—'

'Talking of the poor—which I suppose includes her,' Richard said, laughing, 'I saw old Granny Hayne snitch a couple of apples when she hoped no one was looking.'

'Did she really?' Hannah was amused.

'And there's another thing.'

Irene was in a thoroughly bad temper. As they were leaving the church, saying goodbye to William Weston in the porch, Mary Eversley had buttonholed her to inquire how Hannah was after the accident at the Drivers'. Mary had commented that it was a pity that Hannah had insisted on riding Vain Glory when she was so inexperienced and unable to control the horse.

'That mad chap, Nick Hayne, walking up and down the aisle and shaking hands with people,' she continued. 'Everyone says he's just a simpleton—what we used to call a mental defective—and quite harmless, but I'm not so sure.' She glanced at Hannah, but decided to continue. 'And now he's not a child any more. He's in his twenties, a grown man, and in my opinion no one can be sure he couldn't be dangerous, given the right—or wrong—circumstances. I'll never understand why they let him out of that asylum place—'mental homes', they call them now, don't they?—to live with his grandmother.'

'He gives me the creeps,' Hannah said.

'I should stay away from him, if I were you,' advised her father.

'It's not always possible, you know, Dad.'

'No,' Irene agreed, 'not when he's allowed to wander around everywhere—even in church. I think you should speak to Weston about him, Richard.'

'It wouldn't do any good. Weston's spoken to the grandmother, and he got told off good and proper. She said if he was a real Christian he'd be glad to have Nick come to his church, and if Christ had to choose between him and her Nick she knew what would happen. And there was a lot more. Poor William was thankful to get away from her.'

'Poor William indeed!' Irene could not be placated. 'He does love the sound of his own voice. I thought his sermon would never come to an end.'

At that moment the Reverend William Weston had retired to St Michael's vicarage, where he was sitting in a comfortable armchair, his feet on a stool, sipping a pre-luncheon glass of sherry. His wife sat opposite him, knitting a garment for a grandchild. The door of the sitting-room was open, and an appetizing smell of roast beef reached him from the kitchen. One of their daughters, home for the weekend, had undertaken to cook the Sunday meal. This was a favourite time of his, when he relaxed and reviewed the success or otherwise of the morning service he had just conducted. But today he was not at ease.

'Something worrying you, William?' Gail Weston asked.

'I was wondering, my dear, if you could have a word with old Mrs Hayne?'

'What about?' It was an unnecessary question; she knew the answer.

'About her grandson, of course.' Weston was not deceived by his wife's seeming ignorance. Unconsciously echoing Irene Aston, he said, 'Nick's not a child any more. He's become such a great big lumbering figure that people are beginning to find him disturbing. Bill Eversley suggested to me that we should stop him making a nuisance of himself in the church. Intentionally or not, he disrupts the service whenever he feels like it.'

'I thought you'd already spoken to Granny Hayne.' Gail Weston consulted her knitting pattern.

'I did, but that was some time ago, and I must admit my intervention had no effect. But he's getting worse. I'm sure he literally frightens some of the younger members of the congregation. I saw that little Aston girl—Hannah—carefully step to one side to avoid him, and it seemed to me that she gave him a very doubtful look. Gail, you don't think she could possibly have heard that he once killed a girl, do you? We know it was said to be accidental and he was provoked. The girl had laughed at him and taunted him with being mental, but—but he did kill her. He'd probably have gone to prison instead of to that mental home if he hadn't been fourteen at the time.'

'I sincerely hope Hannah Aston hasn't heard.' Gail put down her knitting; her husband had now got her full attention. 'William, if that story gets around, his life will be impossible, and so will his grandmother's. She may have a sharp tongue, but she's almost eighty and she's dependent on him, whatever his background. It would be very sad for both of them.'

'I know.' Weston hesitated. 'So will you speak to her?'

Mrs Weston sighed. 'All right, I'll try,' she said.

CHAPTER 4

Monday was one of those autumn days when the Cotswolds are at their best, the air crisp, the skies clear, the leaves turning gold to russet brown to red before they fall. In spite of herself, Hannah's spirits were lifted by the weather as she set off for Coriston College. At this time of year the lanes were comparatively free of motor traffic and she cycled at a leisurely pace, enjoying the ride.

It took her about twenty minutes to reach the college, which had once been a Georgian mansion belonging to the Coriston family, now long extinct. The main building, though greatly altered and known as School House, remained; it was here, at the nucleus of the school, that the headmaster had his residence and the building also contained the Assembly Hall and the administrative facilities. Six boarding-houses had been built in the extensive grounds. The school chapel was nearby and the science laboratories, a gymnasium and a covered swimming pool were grouped together a little further away from the main building.

Not yet a hundred years old, Coriston—pronounced 'Corston' by those in the know—College was one of many such Victorian establishments and could hardly be classed as among England's greatest public schools. Nevertheless, it had a good reputation for its academic work, as well as its sport and its extracurricular activities, such as music and drama. But most especially it was renowned for its homelike atmosphere and the individual care given to each pupil. For this reason it had become popular with parents living abroad who needed or merely desired to send their children home to school; the fact that it was co-educational and therefore brothers and sisters could be close to each other was another point in its favour. After a poor period, during which there had been something of a scandal and later a change of headmaster, Coriston was again flourishing. This was reflected in its fees.

Hannah, who had hated the comprehensive school in Colombury to which she had first been sent when the Astons returned from Germany, had been delighted by the move to Coriston and had found herself well-suited to the College, albeit as a day girl. But today, as she came to the big wrought iron gates and started to cycle up the long tree-lined drive, she experienced no pleasure.

She put her bicycle away in the shed behind School House and, kicking at fallen leaves, walked across to Browne's, where she shared a study with Marjorie Eversley; at Coriston sixth-form day pupils had at least shared studies. Marjorie had not yet arrived, but Monica Vaughan, the senior house prefect, was there.

'Mr Browne wants to see you, Hannah.'

'He does? D'you know why?'

'No idea. He just asked me to give you the message.'

Consoling herself with the thought that whatever it was, it wouldn't take long because there wasn't much time before Assembly, Hannah took off her outdoor clothes and went along to the Housemaster's study. She hesitated before she knocked, to flick back her hair and straighten her shoulders. Now that she was in the sixth form she was no longer required to wear the school uniform, and she was conscious of looking attractive in a pretty white blouse and a calf-length violet-coloured skirt that matched her eyes.

'You wanted to see me, Mr Browne?'

'Yes, Hannah. Come in. Sit down.'

Morgan Browne sat behind his desk. He was already wearing the gown which signified his authority, but he was not a naturally authoritative man. He had brown shaggy hair and large brown eyes which reminded one of a spaniel's, so that it was difficult to imagine anyone hating him or even disliking him. Yet this very disarming attitude, which in fact allowed him to get his own way much of the time, could be infuriating. It often infuriated his wife, Shirley, to such an extent that she had threatened to leave him.

'Hannah,' Morgan Browne began, smiling at her sadly. 'What has happened to you? You used to be one of the brightest and most hard-working of girls. But not this term. I keep on getting complaints about you—essays unfinished on time, work ill-prepared, careless mistakes. The last lot of complaints has come from Mr Blondel, your form master, who has always had a high opinion of you. Have you given up hoping to get a place at Oxford? You know, Mr Blondel once believed you might get a scholarship, which is why he offered to give you extra coaching. But not any more, he tells me. You don't seem to care.'

'I do care,' Hannah said, 'but—'

'But what, my dear?'

Damn Stephen Blondel, Hannah thought, and damn Morgan Browne. Why couldn't they leave her alone? Everyone seemed to be going for her, asking questions, worrying her, as if she didn't have enough problems.

'Are there difficulties at home? Is that it?' Browne persisted. 'Come on, Hannah, you can tell me. We're friends, aren't we?'

'No, there's nothing wrong at home—sir,' Hannah replied.

The 'sir' was intentional—and indeed sounded as if it was meant as a rebuke. The idea that she and Morgan Browne were—or indeed ever had been—*friends* was laughable. But she knew she had to produce some kind of explanation, or he would go on probing. After all, he was her Housemaster.

'I think perhaps I've been doing too much, too many other things, so that my school work's been neglected. I seem to get very tired these days.'

'Oh dear! Perhaps you should see Dr Fenwick. You mustn't let yourself get ill, Hannah.'

'I'm not ill! And I don't want to see the doctor!' Hannah said, her anger barely suppressed. Then she heard the door of the study open behind her and saw Morgan Browne's expression of worried sympathy suddenly become blank. 'I—I'm sorry my work's been poor, Mr Browne. I will try harder.' She turned, knowing that it would be Shirley Browne who had entered the study without knocking, and wondering how much she had overheard. 'May I go now?'

'Yes. Right, Hannah. It's almost time for Assembly.'

'What was all that about?' Shirley Browne asked as Hannah fled, giving her a brief nod that was an apology for a greeting.

'I'm afraid I've been lecturing her about her work, which has deteriorated badly this term. I had to. Stephen Blondel, who has gone out of his way to help her, keeps on complaining to me. Why he can't handle the problem himself, I don't know.'

'Perhaps he thought you would be more forceful,' Shirley said sarcastically. 'Anyway, did you discover from your heart to heart with Miss Hannah why she's lost interest?'

'Not really.'

'I didn't imagine you had. If it had been some plain child you'd have been fine—kind, fatherly, but very firm. But with a sexy little piece like Hannah Aston you—'

'Shirley, please!'

'Well, it's true, Morgan. There's something strange about that girl. She's knowing, and yet . . . ' Shirley shrugged. 'I expect she's having trouble with her boyfriend, and that's the problem.'

'I didn't even know she had a boyfriend.'

Shirley gave her husband a long, amused glance, but made no answer. In the distance a bell sounded. Morgan Browne pushed back his chair and stood up, relieved that the summons to Assembly gave him an impeccable excuse for cutting short a conversation that he had found increasingly disturbing and unpleasing.

'I must go,' he said.

'Of course,' Shirley agreed; she couldn't have sounded less involved.

Hannah knew that Morgan Browne was right. Undoubtedly she had been neglecting her work. She couldn't concentrate, and somehow none of it seemed to matter. She couldn't believe it was worthwhile to make the effort. The idea of going up to Oxford—or any other university—was no longer real—and she didn't care. The immediate future was what was important.

She went through the morning in a dream, scarcely listening to what was being taught, and earning more than one reprimand from Stephen Blondel. Blondel, who had joined the staff at the beginning of the summer term straight from university with a good English degree, was a pleasant, fresh-faced young man whose poor eyesight had caused him to fail at all sports and given him an inferiority complex which he disguised behind a supercilious manner. A little afraid of the more senior of the classes he taught, where the pupils were not so much younger than himself, he tended to treat them as equals at one moment and as children the next. This characteristic hadn't made him popular.

Hannah, who had started by being one of his favourites, partly because she had shown herself to be genuinely interested in English literature and partly because he was attracted to her, had since her fall from grace suffered in particular from his caustic and often witty comments. As a result, whereas she had once admired Stephen Blondel, she now disliked him and, when she could be bothered, occasionally got her own back by being insolent to the point of rudeness.

Immediately after lunch this Monday, before afternoon classes had begun, she told Marjorie that she wasn't feeling too well and was going over to the sanatorium to report to Matron. To Matron she said she had a sick headache and Matron, used to declarations of ill-health which could be either genuine or false, had regarded her seriously for a full minute.

'Yes,' she said at last, 'You do look a bit peaky, Hannah.'

'Peaky' was a word that Irene Aston used, and for a moment Hannah was ashamed of the lie she had told. 'I—I'd like to go home,' she muttered.

'Is it your period?' Matron asked.

'Yes,' Hannah lied. 'It's just started.'

'Then I think it would be best if you lay down for a while and I gave you a couple of paracetamol.' Matron was firm.

Hannah made no attempt to argue. In fact, it suited her purpose not to leave Coriston too early. She took the tablets, thanked Matron and went to lie down in a small room off the san. When Matron looked in an hour later she said she felt much better, but would still like to go home.

'All right,' Matron agreed; she never felt the same responsibility for the day students as for the boarders. 'But if you're getting regular trouble ask your mother to take you to Dr Fenwick—or you can see him here at the school.'

'Yes, Matron, and thank you,' Hannah said meekly.

She had no intention of seeing Dr Fenwick or of mentioning this incident to her mother. Indeed she had no intention of going home, at least not directly.

When her father had said over breakfast that he had some business to do in Oxford for the British Legion that day, and her mother had immediately said that she would go with him to do a little shopping, Hannah had seen her opportunity. Her parents were predictable. They didn't go into Oxford very often, but when they did they always had tea—and Richard insisted on a drink—at the Randolph before driving home. She could count on them not being back until six-thirty at the earliest. And she had made a plan.

Ignoring the lane that led to their house, Hannah rode straight on to Colombury. She propped her bicycle against the wall beside the premises of Merger & Son, Wine and Spirit Merchants, and was locking it when she was hailed by name. Rodney Driver had just come out of the shop.

'Hello, Hannah, what are you doing here? Playing truant from Coriston?'

'Certainly not!'

'Well, how are you, sweetie? Recovered from that horrid fall on Saturday, I hope. It got quite a write-up in our local rag today.'

'More or less. I'm still a bit bruised. More important, how's Vain Glory? I haven't seen the newspaper.'

'Not too good. He's horribly lame.' Driver shook his head sadly. 'And I gather that, to add to our grief, you're abandoning us. Your mama is mightily displeased—so no more riding lessons with the Drivers. I shall miss you.'

'I'm sorry about Glory,' Hannah said, disregarding the rest of Rodney Driver's remarks.

'I suppose we couldn't persuade your mama to change her mind, could we?' Driver glanced at his watch. 'I know it's early, but what about a spot of tea at the Windrush so that we can consider the problem?'

'There's no problem. I've given up riding, and I don't mind in the least.' Hannah spoke definitely. 'Now, if you'll excuse me, I'll say goodbye, Rodney.'

'*Au revoir*, Hannah,' said Driver, and thought that one of these days the little bitch was going to pay for her uppishness.

Hannah, unaware of Driver's venomous thoughts, had gone into the Mergers' store. Peter was alone behind the counter. He mimed surprise.

'What can I do for you, madam? I saw you being chatted up by our *chevalier sans peur et sans reproche*, but I didn't expect you to enter my humble portals.'

'Hello, Peter. Don't be a fool. I'd like half a bottle of gin, please.'

'Gin? But, madam, you're under age to buy hard liquor. However, I've a nice line in ginger ale if you're interested.'

'For goodness sake, do stop fooling, Peter. It's a present for Dad.'

'Christmas is a long way off.'

'It's for his birthday.'

'When is it? Because if it's before November 1st he'll find a half bottle of gin on his end of month account, and won't that surprise him?'

'I'll pay for it.'

Peter put his head on one side and regarded Hannah dubiously. He sensed that she was nervous and wondered why. Could the gin possibly be for some boyfriend and not for her father? He hesitated before serving her, but . . .

'OK. What brand would you like?'

'Gordon's. It's what Dad usually drinks, isn't it?' Hannah said guilelessly.

Peter grinned. 'That's right. It's what he orders, anyway. He found the half-bottle for which she had asked, and was about to put it into a Mergers' carrier bag when she stopped him. 'What's the matter?'

'Haven't you a plain bag? I don't want to advertise the fact I've been buying liquor.'

'Of course not! What would your mummy say? She might accuse you of consorting with that common Merger boy again.'

Hannah glared at him and plonked the money down on the counter. Peter, after a considerable search, found a plain white bag, and put the gin in it.

'There you are,' he said, passing it to her. 'Is that all right?'

'Thank you.'

For a moment they smiled at each other, both thinking of what might have been, both knowing they could never return to their former relationship. Then, with a wave of her hand, she left the shop. She turned back at once.

'Peter, that horrible Nick Hayne's examining my bike.'

'Nick Hayne's OK, Hannah. He won't hurt you.'

'How do you know? You don't!' Hannah was suddenly angry. 'He may not be responsible for his actions, but the end result is the same. The fact that he didn't mean it won't help anyone he does hurt.' She stopped abruptly.

'Has he ever hurt you?' Peter looked at her curiously. He still retained a protective feeling for the girl.

'No—o,' Hannah said sulkily.

'Well then . . . ' Peter said, but he came from behind the counter and went to the door of the shop to look out. 'Anyway, he's gone, Hannah. He's way up the road, disappearing into the distance. You're quite safe now.'

Although she knew Peter was mocking her, Hannah

didn't react. She smiled at him, said, 'Thanks a lot, Peter,' and went. Frowning thoughtfully, Peter Merger watched her unlock her bicycle and ride away.

Major and Mrs Aston returned home rather later than usual, having had some trouble with their car's ignition. They found the house in darkness. But there was a note on the kitchen table which read, '*Have gone to bed with sick headache. Please don't disturb. Will be all right in morning. Love. Hannah.*'

Of course Irene Aston couldn't resist the temptation to peep into her daughter's room but, seeing by the light in the passage Hannah's sleeping form and hearing her steady snores, she withdrew, satisfied.

CHAPTER 5

It was three o'clock the following morning and Hannah was puking her heart out. Irene was standing beside her, offering a damp towel for her head, paper tissues to wipe her mouth, flushing the toilet. Richard hovered uncertainly in the doorway, asking if he should phone the doctor. Hannah felt too ill to appreciate their concern, but she knew that she did not want to see Dr Fenwick.

'No, Dad! No!' She felt as if she were screaming though in fact her voice emerged as a hoarse croak. 'Must be something I ate yesterday. Sorry.'

Her mother went to the bathroom door and Hannah became aware of her parents conferring together. She tried to protest again that she didn't want or need a doctor, but her stomach heaved and once more she was vomiting. She had never felt so ghastly in her life, and she wondered if she might be about to collapse and die. At least that would solve all her problems. But the spasm passed and she was left breathing heavily.

Irene returned. 'Your father's gone to phone Dr Fenwick. I'm sure he'll come. You can't go on being sick like this or you'll get dehydrated.'

Hannah accepted that it was too late to argue, though she was now feeling a little better. This, however, proved to be temporary and she was vomiting again, or to be more exact trying to vomit from an empty stomach when the doctor arrived.

'Sounds like food poisoning from your description,' he said to Irene. 'It only needs the smallest scrap of tainted meat or fish to cause it.'

Dr Kenneth Fenwick was in his late thirties, a short, square man with a hearty manner. He was one of the junior partners of Dr Dick Band, who had had a flourishing practice in Colombury for many years. As Colombury had grown, so had the practice, and now there were four partners sharing the work, though Band himself acted as the police surgeon, while Fenwick took special responsibility for the staff and pupils of Coriston College.

Fenwick examined Hannah briefly. He smelt her breath, but made no comment. 'I'm going to give you an injection to try to settle your insides, Hannah,' he said. 'It'll also help you to sleep.'

Turning to Irene, he produced three or four sachets. 'As soon as she can keep anything down mix the contents of one of these with fresh water and make her sip it. It's only salt and glucose, but it'll prevent dehydration better than anything. There'll be no school for her in the morning, so she can have a long lie-in. She should be OK by Wednesday.'

'All right, doctor. And thanks.'

Hannah, who had heard all this, smiled wanly and echoed her mother's thanks. The idea of bed and sleep was enticing. She didn't care about school. Indeed the excuse she had given Matron to enable her to cut classes the previous afternoon would now be validated. No one, not even Shirley Browne could have cause for complaint once her mother, supported by Dr Fenwick, had telephoned to explain her absence. The thought pleased her. But otherwise her orgy of gin had been a waste of effort. There was no sign of her period starting. Nothing, she thought bitterly, was going to rid her of the damned baby except a proper abortion.

As Dr Fenwick had predicted, by Wednesday Hannah had got over her sickness and was feeling comparatively well. She insisted on cycling to Coriston though Richard volunteered to drive her. As she was walking from the bicycle shed to Browne's she met a group of runners from Condor's House, among them Alan Carson and Ian Merger.

'Hello, Hannah,' called Alan. 'Are you better?' He and Ian stopped.

'Yes, thanks, Alan. Just a spot of food poisoning. Nothing serious,' Hannah replied, doing her best to sound casual.

'Oh dear!' Alan was amused. 'You do seem to be accident-prone at present—what with losing control of Vain Glory, and now food poisoning!' The remark was not made kindly.

Ian laughed. 'That's two lucky escapes, Hannah. What will the third be? You'd better take care. Incidentally, did you see what our local paper had to say about your horsemanship? Not very flattering, was it?'

Hannah drew a deep breath. At her comprehensive school she had learnt some swear words and obscene curses that would have shocked her parents, and which she was sure Alan Carson would never have heard, though Ian Merger probably had. Luckily she was saved from uttering them.

A peremptory voice said, 'Cut along, Hannah. And you boys, hurry up!'

The speaker was Stanley Tranter, Coriston's Head of School, a scholar and a fine athlete, a Cambridge scholarship already under his belt. A tall, willowy young man with a sardonic expression, he appeared more sophisticated than he was. But he was generally liked, though he had a few detractors.

Alan muttered an imprecation under his breath, but he and Ian obeyed, and Hannah went on her way to Browne's. She found Marjorie Eversley in the study. Marjorie, unlike the two boys, was genuinely sympathetic.

'Poor Hannah,' she said, 'that was too bad. Still, I'm glad it was only food poisoning and you're better. I was afraid you might have caught a bug—there's a lot of flu going around—and you might miss the Hallowe'en party on Saturday.'

'No, it was just something I'd eaten,' Hannah said, wondering how often she would have to tell this lie.

Marjorie continued to talk about the party and how her bat costume was almost finished. Hannah tried to respond, but she wasn't interested. She was studying her timetable. She had two periods of English before break, then German, followed by physical exercise or gym. Once she would have considered this a good morning, except for the gym to which she was indifferent. Today she had no inclination to be taught anything, and she feared Stephen Blondel's sharp tongue if she appeared bored and listless—which was precisely how she felt. And exercise was the last thing she wanted.

In the event, Blondel—like Marjorie—was sympathetic. He didn't complain about her ill-prepared work or make any remark when her attention seemed to wander, so that she warmed towards him. And the German mistress, who liked Hannah, was always lenient with her; indeed, Hannah had been known to remark that the German lessons were not sufficiently demanding. Today, however, she was thankful to be able to let her thoughts roam.

This, however, was not possible during gym. Beth Price, one of the junior games mistresses, was a diminutive figure, little more than five feet in height, with fair hair and blue eyes, who inspired erotic thoughts in many of the boys and even a couple of masters. Like so many small people she was energetic, enthusiastic and something of a martinet.

'Come on, girls! Come on! Knees higher!' she encouraged as they ran on the spot. 'You're all half asleep. Wake up! This is meant to be a warming-up exercise. Come on! Hannah, you're not trying. Get your knees up.'

It was true that Hannah was not trying. The ankle she had hurt in her fall from Vain Glory was still slightly painful, and she had no desire to do it any further harm. But the real reason was lethargy, and as the session progressed she brought down several more caustic comments on herself. She was thankful when the period was over. And she cut her afternoon classes, which included drama with Shirley Browne, and went home, making the excuse that she was still not feeling well.

'That girl's becoming a damned nuisance!' Shirley was vehement. 'If she thinks she can cut drama class when she chooses and then expect a major part in the school play because of her beautiful hair, like last year, she can think again.'

'Oh, Hannah's not a bad little actress, Shirley,' Morgan said mildly. 'She deserves a good part.'

The Brownes were in the sitting-room of their flat. It was after supper, a time during which they drank their coffee, and possibly had a drink if a colleague was coming in. This evening Shirley was arranging glasses on a side table so it was clear to Morgan that visitors were expected.

'You know,' said Shirley suddenly, 'Beth and I agree.' Shirley and the games mistress were friends. 'There really is something odd about that girl. I suppose it's due to her background. Over-ambitious mother and underachieving father, so that there's not enough money to fulfil all their aspirations. I mean, why does she need riding lessons? Audrey Driver told me the Astons were very slow paying their bills.'

'Shirley, for Heaven's sake!' Morgan protested. 'That's none of our business and you're not a psychiatrist, so stop trying to analyse Hannah Aston.'

'OK. Mustn't say anything against dear Hannah, must we?' Shirley said sarcastically.

There was no time for Morgan to make a riposte. Any further argument was interrupted by a knock at the door, and Shirley said, 'I expect that's Beth now. I asked her to drop in for a drink.'

Morgan sighed. It wasn't that he disliked Beth Price, but he didn't want to get involved in any more discussion of Hannah Aston. Recently Shirley seemed determined to find fault with the girl. But he wasn't sure whether to be pleased or otherwise when, not Beth Price, but Stephen Blondel came in. He liked Blondel and thought him an acquisition for Coriston and Browne's, in spite of his being unsure of himself and having difficulty in dealing with some of his pupils,but he wanted no further complaints about Hannah's work.

'Hello, Stephen,' Morgan welcomed him. 'The drinks are ready. What can we offer you?'

'Nothing, thanks. I'd love to, but I've a pile of sixth-form essays to correct before tomorrow and, as it is, I can see I'll be up long past midnight.'

Stephen Blondel smothered a yawn, apologizing to Shirley. He had never realized until he started teaching how exhausting that occupation could be. And some of the students he found difficult to deal with; the more senior girls were inclined to tease, the boys to mock, and he was never quite sure . . . Sometimes he wondered if he had been wise to accept a post a Coriston, but a First Class Honours degree in English from Oxford didn't qualify one for many jobs these days, and at the time he had been thankful for the position when it was offered to him.

'Stephen's come to collect the headgear you wore last Hallowe'en, you know, that funny kind of hood, Morgan. I said you'd lend it to him,' Shirley remarked.

'Of course. Shirley's made me a splendid new one, so you can keep the old one if you like.'

'Many thanks.'

'I'll just get it,' Shirley said. 'I won't be a minute, Stephen.'

'It's very kind of you and Shirley,' Stephen said. 'To be honest I'm not looking forward to this party. I'm not much good at dancing, I'm afraid, or anything else in the athletic line for that matter, as you know.'

'I shouldn't worry.' Morgan laughed. 'The whole thing's a bit of a shambles really, but luckily it's only once a year —something to be enjoyed or endured.'

Shirley returned with a carrier bag as the two men grinned together. 'I've put in some matching gloves, Stephen. Are you sure you won't change your mind and have a drink with us?'

'Quite sure, but thanks for the offer. And many thanks for the fancy headgear. I trust it'll fit easily over my spectacles.'

He had scarcely left when Beth Price arrived, and once again the conversation turned to Hannah Aston. Whether from tact or conviction Miss Price's opinion seemed to be similar to Mrs Browne's. Morgan contributed little. He didn't want another argument with his wife, especially in front of Beth Price. Coriston was a small community, and inevitably gossip and rumour were well fed. However, Morgan Browne could take only so much of what he considered the women's bitchiness. Abruptly he stood up and said, 'If you'll excuse me, I have some work to do.'

He heard his wife starting to apologize for him as he left the room. Later, he knew, he and Shirley would have a full-blown row. It seemed to him that they were always having rows these days.

Two days later, on Friday afternoon, Morgan Browne went into Oxford to visit his dentist; for some time he had been having trouble with a wisdom tooth. The matter dealt with satisfactorily, he took the opportunity to do some early Christmas shopping and then decided to have tea before returning to Coriston.

He was making his way to a pleasant café that he knew in Ship Street when he saw Hannah Aston standing at a bus stop. He nearly passed by, but either her dejected stance or the woebegone droop of her head stopped him. He crossed the road to her.

'Hello, Hannah. What are you doing here on a Friday afternoon?'

'I—I—' She was obviously startled by his appearance, and it seemed to Browne as if she was fumbling for an excuse. 'I had to come to the dentist,' she lied. In fact, she had made a tentative visit to an abortion clinic, but had been horrified at the number of questions the nurse-receptionist had asked, She had expected everything to be simple. She hadn't foreseen the amount of money that would be required in advance of the operation or that they would want her to stay overnight. She knew she couldn't cope with these complications by herself and, waiting her turn for the doctor's preliminary examination, she had suddenly panicked and walked out.

'That's a coincidence! So did I,' said Browne. Even then he would have left her, but close to she looked miserable and ill. He thought of the long ride back to Colombury she would face on a bus that meandered around innumerable villages, and he said, 'Hannah, I was just going to have a cup of tea. If you'd like to join me I could give you a lift home afterwards.'

'Oh, thank you. That would be wonderful.' Hannah was genuinely grateful. She too knew Cotswold buses.

Morgan Browne tucked his hand under her elbow and led her back across the road. Neither of them noticed Audrey Driver, who watched them go into the café with surprised interest.

Tea seemed to cheer Hannah, but Browne did most of the talking, carefully avoiding any contentious subject. They didn't linger and soon, leaving the café, they were in the Brownes' Ford Fiesta and heading out of Oxford.

They were about a mile from the outskirts of Colombury when the engine coughed, the car jerked forward a couple of yards and came to a standstill. Morgan Browne swore. He looked at the petrol gauge and tried the ignition, but without result. He got out of the car, opened the bonnet and peered at the engine. By now it was dark. Even if he had known what to look for, he wouldn't have been able to see it. The words he muttered under his breath were not what he would have wanted Hannah to hear—or Shirley, for that matter. He was, he knew, in a damnable mess.

It was not too warm and he got back into the car. They would have to wait until they could hitch a ride. But this stretch of road was not popular and it was some while before they saw the lights of an approaching vehicle. He stepped into the road and waved his arms wildly. The van drove past, but then braked sharply. Peter Merger got out and walked back to Morgan Browne's car.

'Mr Browne? Hi! You've broken down? Then we're well met. You'd like a lift to Coriston?'

'No. To Danforth's garage, if you will. They'll cope with my car and take me on. Luckily it's not far.'

Suddenly Browne was aware that Merger had stiffened and was looking past him to the Ford. A wry expression crossed his face. Browne turned. Hannah had got out of his car and was coming towards them.

'And where shall I take Miss Aston, sir?' Merger asked, no longer friendly and cooperative, but over-polite, if not actually sarcastic.

Morgan Browne felt the colour rush into his cheeks. He hoped it was too dark for Merger to notice. He gritted his teeth and was reminded that he had been to the dentist, but he was damned if he was going to offer the Merger youth any explanations.

'Perhaps you'd be good enough to drop her at her house,' he said, regretting that he should sound so pompous.

'Certainly—sir. I'm afraid three people in the front of the van aren't going to be too comfortable, but fortunately it's only a short ride.'

And indeed Peter Merger was right. It *was* uncomfortable. It was also embarrassing and more or less silent. Morgan Browne was dropped off at the garage, and Hannah and Peter headed for Hannah's house.

'The bottom of the lane will be fine,' said Hannah.

'OK.' Peter didn't argue. He leant across and opened the door of the van for her, but didn't get out. 'Good night.'

'Good night. Thanks for the lift.' Hannah was equally distant.

Hannah Aston told her parents that she had been kept late at school, reading for the play, and Mr Blondel, who had been going into Colombury, had brought her to the end of the lane. She didn't want them to know she had been to Oxford.

Morgan Browne didn't tell his wife a direct lie. But he did not mention meeting Hannah Aston, giving her tea and offering to drive her home. He didn't want yet another row.

Audrey Driver kept her own counsel.

Peter Merger also kept a discreet silence. He didn't want to listen to any more disparaging remarks about Hannah from his mother, who believed the Astons were a snobbish family without any justification, and that the girl had treated her son badly.

CHAPTER 6

Hallowe'en. A night when witches fly across the sky on broomsticks, bats flutter and screech, devils appear and disappear in puffs of smoke, ghosties and ghoulies glide about, mischievous spirits are abroad and even pumpkins have been known to walk. A night for fun and games, for tricks and treats, a night to be enjoyed, perhaps. And this particular Hallowe'en was an unseasonably warm night—the weather had suddenly changed—and there was a moon that played hide and seek behind clouds to provide an appropriate atmosphere.

Hannah Aston sat behind Marjorie Eversley on the back seat of the Astons' car; it had been agreed that Richard should drive the girls to the party at Coriston, and Bill Eversley would collect them and take them home. For once Marjorie looked the more attractive of the two. The black net threaded with silver that had once been a pretty evening dress had been transformed by Mary Eversley into a charming bat costume which flattered Marjorie's skinny frame.

Compared to her Hannah looked tatty. Irene had pressed the scarlet skirt and mended the pointed black hat that hid Hannah's hair, but the total effect was nondescript and uninteresting.

Not that Hannah cared. She was going to the party only because it was easier than to invent an excuse for not going. But she was nervous. She had made up her mind that she must confide in her father, and she would do so this evening. Time was passing, and something had to be done soon. On the way to Coriston she scarcely volunteered a remark, while Marjorie prattled.

'The church fair today was a great success, wasn't it, Major? Mum said they made loads of money, but it was a lot of work for all the helpers, and she's glad it's over till next year. I expect Mrs Aston feels much the same.'

'Indeed she does, Marjorie. It's been an exhausting day for everyone concerned. But this is a busy time of year. There's still the poppy appeal to come, and Remembrance Day.'

'Yes. And Bonfire Night,' Marjorie said, unaware that she had vaguely offended Major Aston by her casual connection of Guy Fawkes with the British Legion. 'Then it'll be the Christmas holidays,' she went on. 'My brothers will be home and there'll be parties and dances. I'm hoping to persuade Dad to let us give a dance. You'd come, wouldn't you, Hannah?'

'If I'm asked,' Hannah said shortly, thinking it unlikely that she would be going to any parties or dances at Christmas.

But by now they had reached Coriston, and Marjorie, who had been rebuffed by Hannah's cool reception of her news about the dance, became talkative again. She enthused about the fairy lights on the trees that lined the drive, though in fact they did little to illuminate the scene. She expressed delight at the big candlelit pumpkin, waiting to welcome the party-goers by the front door of School House. Various shadowy forms were entering the building.

'You go ahead, Marjorie,' Hannah said suddenly as Richard drew up. 'There's something I want to ask Dad.'

'All right.' Marjorie was none too pleased, but she got out of the car. 'See you in the cloakroom. Thank you for the lift, Major.'

'What is it, Hannah?' Richard asked when Marjorie had gone.

'I've something to tell you, Dad. I can't tell Mum because she'd never stop asking questions that I couldn't answer, and it would drive me mad. I—I'd rather kill myself!'

'Hannah! For God's sake, what is it?' Richard was appalled. 'I thought it was something unimportant, money perhaps, or you wanted a new dress for a party that your mother wouldn't approve of, or—' His imagination failed. 'Are you in some kind of trouble, real trouble?'

'Yes, I am—in desperate trouble.'

Richard Aston twisted around in the driver's seat in an attempt to see his daughter's face, but Hannah had pulled down her witch's mask. All he could see in the unilluminated back of the car was a grotesque image, Moreover, the mask distorted Hannah's voice so that he was unable to judge if, as she sounded, she was on the verge of tears.

'What a time to choose to tackle me about whatever it is!' He didn't mean to be unsympathetic, but he was at a loss. 'I don't understand.'

'I'm telling you now, Dad, so that you can go away and think about it—think what I'm to do. I've run out of ideas myself or I wouldn't have told you.'

'Hannah, darling one, you haven't told me anything yet.'

'And you're sure you've not guessed, Dad? Well, I'll put it into plain words for you. *I'm pregnant*, and I won't—I can't—have the baby.'

*

In the Assembly Hall—transformed for the night into an approximation of a sophisticated nightclub—the disco party had been under way for some time. The so-called *Coriston Cherubs* were banging away at the latest pop tune and the floor was crowded with dancers. Some of the older staff were sitting out, others had gone to find an illegal quiet drink in the staff room or to sample the food which was laid out in a separate room. Yet others were trying to keep an unofficial eye on the younger members of the school—an impossible task.

'What's wrong with this shindig,' said Alan Carson, 'is that there's no liquor, not even shandy. How can one have a proper party with only lemonade and orangeade and suchlike to drink?'

'It's a pity, but unluckily there's nothing we can do about it,' Ian Merger said.

'That's where you're wrong!' Alan was triumphant. 'I foresaw this difficulty last weekend and raided my father's cellar. I've made a nice little cache under the games pavilion.'

'It's a fair way to go in the dark,' Ian demurred.

'So what? You're not scared?'

'Of course not!'

A few minutes later two figures, one in a green body suit, the other in red, emerged from a side door of School House and disappeared into the night. They had almost reached their objective—the wine hidden beneath the pavilion—when a car with no lights shot out from the trees that surrounded the main playing field and screeched across it. Both boys flung themselves out of the vehicle's path.

'Ian, are you OK?' Alan demanded, as the car bumped on to the drive and was gone.

'Yes. Sure. And you, Alan? You saw who was driving?'

'Yes, I did. The moon came out just at the right moment.

But I should think we'd better keep our mouths shut. It's none of our business and we don't want to have to explain what *we* were doing here, do we?'

'I'll say not! OK, Alan. We forget it.'

At about this time, or perhaps a little later, two forms wrapped in a thick cloak lay entwined in a far corner of the shrubbery on the further side of the playing field. They were Stanley Tranter, the Head of School, and Monica Vaughan, the senior prefect of Browne's House. Monica's blouse was undone to the waist so that her breasts were exposed, and she had unzipped Stanley's fly and pulled down his trousers. They had been kissing and fondling each other for some while. They were both aroused.

'Come on, Moni. Let me,' Stanley whispered. 'I want you properly, and you know you want me. We've both been yearning for a chance like this for ages. Let me.'

'No, Stan. Not all the way.'

'Why not? You're not a virgin.'

'No, but—'

'But what? Moni, Moni, I can feel that you're ready for me. Come on.'

He was on the point of pulling up her skirt and thrusting himself into her when she suddenly pushed him violently away, and involuntarily he ejaculated over their clothes and the cloak. 'Damn you!' he said. 'Damn you!'

'Be quiet!' she hissed. 'There's someone else in the shrubbery. Listen!'

Stanley didn't believe it. Furiously angry and frustrated, he rolled off her, sat up and started to clean himself as best he could and rearrange his clothing. Then he too heard the rustle of leaves, the noise made by someone moving quietly through the undergrowth. Who?

Monica was doing up her brassière and buttoning her blouse, breathing nervously. Both of them were thinking of the consequences if they were caught. What they did in the holidays was their parents' business. Term-time was different; neither of them wanted to end their years at Coriston in disgrace.

But the sounds were retreating. Stanley Tranter stood up carefully and dusted himself down. He thought of his father, who himself enjoyed a succession of mistresses but wouldn't have approved of his son's present behaviour. He cursed under his breath as he gave Monica a hand and pulled her to her feet.

'Shall I go first, or you?'

'Can't we go together?' she said nervously.

Reluctantly Stanley agreed, and they began to move cautiously through the shrubbery in the direction of the main building. Then, when they felt almost safe, a white ghost-like figure suddenly loomed before them. Monica screamed. Stanley drew a sharp breath, and the thought crossed his mind that they would have to make some excuse for their presence outside and hope they would be believed. But before he could think of one the 'ghost' turned and fled.

When Monica Vaughan reached the School House she went straight to the cloakroom to tidy herself and regain her composure. There she found Hannah, Marjorie and Shirley Browne, who had all temporarily removed their disguises. Hannah was pinning up her hair which had come loose under her witch's hat, and Mrs Browne, dressed as a demon, was doing a quick repair on Marjorie's bat costume which she had torn.

'Hello, who are you?' Shirley asked.

Monica, another witch, took off her mask and greeted them. She dropped the soiled cloak on to a bench, but no one took any notice of it or of her stained skirt. Hannah went, in spite of Marjorie's request to wait for her, and as she left, in came a ghost. For a moment Monica felt chilled;

then she realized that ghosts were two a penny at a Hallowe'en party; this petite figure could not be the same as the one she had encountered with Stanley.

The ghost removed its headgear, fashioned from a pillowcase, and revealed the broadly smiling face of Beth Price, the games mistress. 'You'll never guess what I've been doing,' she said.

'What?' Shirley asked, completing her repair on Marjorie's costume.

'I've been trying to teach poor Stephen Blondel to dance. You can't imagine anyone less well-coordinated. He just hasn't a clue. No sense of rhythm and no control of his limbs, though he tried awfully hard.' Beth couldn't stop laughing. 'To crown everything, I trod on his tail and it came off, so I had to pin it back on for him.'

The others joined in her amusement. Marjorie thanked Shirley Browne for her efforts and departed to the hall. The two older women soon followed her. Monica, left alone, hurriedly did her best to wash the stains left by Stanley from her skirt and the cloak. She felt she had had a lucky escape, but she was still worried about the 'ghost' who had seen them outside.

The Hallowe'en party ended at midnight. The Headmaster, Dr Peregrine Sheringham, and Mrs Sheringham, who wore plain evening dress, distributed the prizes. In his late fifties, by far the oldest of the staff of Coriston College, Dr Sheringham was an austere character and many had thought him a strange choice when his predecessor had moved to another school. But he had become generally liked, and had proved himself surprisingly understanding of the problems of both staff and students.

He had his doubts about the propriety of the annual Hallowe'en party, but he kept them to himself, accepting that it was a Coriston tradition. He respected traditions, but he always breathed a sigh of relief when the evening was over without any unpleasant aftermath to be regretted.

CHAPTER 7

Richard Aston sat at the kitchen table, a mug of tea in front of him. He had taken up Irene's tray, and knew that very soon she would be coming downstairs to cook breakfast. The previous evening, tired from a long day spent at the church fair, she had gone to bed early and had been asleep when he returned from taking Hannah and Marjorie to the Hallowe'en party.

He had been thankful for this. It had given him more time to compose himself—he had even managed to sleep for a couple of hours—and he hadn't been forced to provide explanations as to why he was so late home and where he had been. He yawned.

Then he heard doors opening and shutting, and steps on the stairs.

He finished his mug of tea as Irene Aston came into the room. 'Richard,' she demanded without preamble, 'have you seen Hannah this morning?'

'No, I haven't. Why? Is she ill?'

'She's not in her room, and her bed looks as if it hasn't been slept in.'

'What?' Richard stared at his wife, remembering Hannah saying that whatever happened Mum must never know. 'She must have gone out, dear. Perhaps she couldn't sleep and decided to go for an early walk—get some fresh air. It's often difficult to sleep properly after a crowded party or a late night. I find the same thing myself.' He stopped, aware that he was talking too much.

'And she carefully made her bed before she went?' Irene's

sarcasm was heavy. How little Richard knew his daughter, she thought. 'Look, Richard,' she said, 'you know as well as I do that Hannah should have been home by twelve-thirty or soon after. Did you hear her come in?'

'No. Did you?'

'No-o.' Irene shook her head slowly. 'There wasn't a note on the kitchen table or anything? If she'd gone out before breakfast she'd have left a note.'

'Irene, be sensible. She may come in at any moment and you know how she hates us to fuss.'

'Yes, but . . . She's never done anything like this before.'

'Done what?'

'Stayed out all night, without us knowing where she was. Don't you care, Richard?'

'Of course I care, my dear. But we don't know that's what she's done. As I say, she may have gone for a breath of fresh air. She'll probably be back soon. Or perhaps she felt unwell at the party. She hasn't been too fit recently, you said yourself—'

'In that case, someone would have let us know.'

'Don't panic, dear. Maybe they didn't want to worry us last night. She could be at the school or with the Eversleys. They'll look after her and phone as soon as they think we'll be up and around. About nine, I expect. We must wait.'

'You could be right, Richard. But I'm worried. I only hope you are.'

From force of habit Irene started to get breakfast, but neither of them wanted much to eat. Hannah's empty place seemed a reproach. When nine-thirty came and still there was no news, Irene refused to wait any longer.

'I'm going to call Morgan Browne,' she said firmly. 'He's her Housemaster, after all. He should know whether or not she's still at Coriston.'

*

The next couple of hours were among the most frustrating that Irene Aston had ever spent.

On phoning Coriston she was informed that neither Mr nor Mrs Browne was available. They had just gone into chapel. On a Sunday there could be a sermon, and the service could last anything from sixty to ninety minutes. If Mrs Aston cared to leave a message . . .

Mrs Aston did care. She would like Mr Browne to telephone her immediately; it was a matter of extreme importance.

Irritated by Mrs Aston's autocratic tone, the housekeeper of Browne's made a note on the pad by the telephone and left it in the hall, where it remained unread until Irene phoned again.

In the meantime Irene tried the Eversleys. Mary Eversley answered. Hannah was not there. Marjorie had arranged to meet Hannah by the front door of School House at the end of the Hallowe'en party, but Hannah hadn't appeared. Marjorie had gone to look for her, without any success. Bill had waited for quite a long time, but when Hannah had still failed to arrive he had reluctantly left the school without her.

'But he promised to bring her home,' Irene expostulated, sounding angry in her anxiety.

'Well, he couldn't wait there all night.' Mary saw no reason why her husband should be blamed. 'Marjorie was tired, over-excited. She needed to get to bed. And if Hannah couldn't keep to the arrangement they had made it was surely her lookout.'

'I don't know what you mean by that, Mary. Hannah must have been somewhere in the building,' Irene persisted, annoyed by what she considered Mary Eversley's indifference. 'She could have been in a lavatory, feeling ill.'

'Marjorie did look for her and, as I said, they waited a long time.' Mary was not to be bullied.

'But surely you could have alerted Mr Browne or someone else at the school, or at least called us when Bill got home without her,' said Irene.

'The place was almost empty when they left and the Brownes had gone to bed, as far as anyone knew. And would you have welcomed a phone call at one-thirty in the morning? Look, Irene, if you want my opinion, Hannah had already left the school last night before Bill and Marjorie were due to meet her.' Mary paused. 'I suppose you haven't called the Mergers, have you?'

'The Mergers? No, why should I?' Irene was genuinely surprised.

'Ian goes home for weekends sometimes, and I thought Peter might have gone to fetch him and offered Hannah a lift. After all, he and Hannah are quite friendly, aren't they?'

Irene clutched the telephone receiver so tightly that her knuckles grew white. She was so angry that she couldn't speak. Silently she cursed Mary and all her family.

'What is it, Irene?' Richard, who had been hovering beside her during the conversation, swallowed hard. 'What is it, Irene?' he repeated, his voice hoarse. 'Hannah?'

Irene shook her head violently. 'Anyway, thanks for your help, Mary.' She forced out the words. 'I'm sorry to have bothered you on a Sunday morning. Please tell Bill not to worry about Hannah. Goodbye.'

She managed to put down the receiver gently, and shocked Richard by the swearing she uttered through clenched teeth. Then she burst into tears and flung herself into his arms. Richard hugged her. He wanted to weep too. He couldn't remember when Irene had last appealed to him like this, whatever the crisis. He patted her on the back and muttered endearments.

And after a minute Irene, whose behaviour was due mainly to her anger with Mary Eversley, got control of herself. 'Those damned Eversleys,' she said. 'Fancy not waiting for her—and then suggesting she might have gone off with the Mergers. Oh, Richard, I'm so afraid Hannah might have started to walk in the hope of hitching a lift and got picked up by some man. One reads such frightful stories in the papers.'

'Which is precisely why Hannah wouldn't do such a stupid thing. She's a sensible girl.' Richard tried to sound encouraging. 'She's most likely at the school, or she's gone with someone she knows and the message telling us has gone astray.'

'She might have borrowed a bicycle to ride home and had an accident.'

'I doubt it. And if there had been an accident, we'd have heard by now.' Richard was becoming slightly impatient; he was under enough of a strain without having to cope with Irene in her present mood. 'My dear, why don't you go and make us some coffee, and I'll phone the Mergers.'

'All right. But make sure you get a straight answer from them.'

'I will,' Richard promised and, thankful to be left alone if only briefly, he tapped out the Mergers' number.

Mrs Merger answered and Richard asked for Peter, saying that he was hoping to persuade him to help with the poppy appeal. But Peter, he was told, was away for a few days and, when he turned the conversation to Ian and Coriston, he learnt that Ian had not come home this weekend as the Hallowe'en party had been late and it had not seemed worth while. Hannah's name was not mentioned.

'So what did the Mergers have to say?' Irene demanded as soon as Richard came into the kitchen.

'Hannah's not there, Irene, but at least we now know that Mary Eversley's suggestion that she went home with the Mergers doesn't hold water,' he said, and recounted the conversation.

'I don't like the Mergers,' Irene admitted, ' but I could wish she *was* there. At least she'd be safe—more or less.' Then in a burst of irritation she added, 'And why on earth don't the Brownes phone?'

Richard looked at his watch. 'They're still in chapel, I suppose,' he said. He hardly believed how early it was. Time had seemed to be galloping past, but in fact it had been crawling and now stretched limitless before them. Poor darling Hannah, he thought, and wondered with dread what the future might hold. Slowly he drank his coffee.

'I assume you don't intend to go to Matins this morning, Irene?' he asked as he put down his cup.

'Without knowing where Hannah is! Certainly not.' Irene hesitated. 'Richard, I've been thinking about Hannah's other friends who aren't boarders. Is it possible that she went off with the Carsons, for instance?'

'Possible, yes—but unlikely.'

'It's equally unlikely that she shouldn't have come home at all last night.' Irene was tart. 'For Heaven's sake, Richard, phone the Brigadier. Why not? He's a friend of yours.'

'All right.'

Richard agreed with some reluctance, but anything was better than sitting and staring at Irene's worried face. Nevertheless, he didn't relish disturbing David Carson on a Sunday morning. Brigadier Carson, retired, worked in the City during the week, and was said to cherish the time he spent at the weekends with his wife, his only son and their frequent house guests. Richard, who knew that Carson had long since ceased to consider him as more than an acquaintance, couldn't help but resent the other man's success and, on the occasions when they met, his patronizing air.

So Richard smiled grimly when the houseman said he would see if Brigadier Carson was available, and it would have been no surprise to him to learn that the gentleman in question was not at home. But Carson came to the phone at once, and seemed full of a kind of angry bonhomie, which at first Richard failed to understand.

'Richard, I know why you've called, old man.' The voice was rich and friendly, but there was suppressed indignation behind it. 'In fact, I was on the point of phoning you to ask after your girl—Hannah, isn't it?—and to get you to join me in writing to the Governors to complain. After all, Coriston may not be the best school in the United Kingdom, but it's meant to pride itself on the care it gives to individual pupils—and its fees are high enough. Don't you agree?'

'I most certainly do.' Richard was trying to discern what on earth Carson was talking about; surely it had to be connected with the Hallowe'en party. 'Actually I was trying to speak to Morgan Browne a little earlier—Hannah's in Browne's house—but everyone seems to have gone to chapel.'

'I know. I've tried to get on to Sheringham myself. It's a pity they don't pay more attention to supervising their students and less attention to praying. That party last night must have been an unholy shambles. Alan was as drunk as a coot when he got home, and my chauffeur says he'd been sick all over the car. In any case, he's paying for it now, poor lad, He's got an almighty hangover.'

'That's too bad.' Richard did his best to sound sympathetic.

'So you'll write and complain, Richard?'

'I'll see what Morgan Browne's got to say, but if it's not satisfactory I'll help you make a hell of a fuss,' Richard promised. 'Must go now, David. Good to have talked to you.' It gave him some satisfaction to be the first to replace the receiver.

'What did Mrs Aston want, Shirley?'

'Well, the trouble seems to be that the Aston girl—Hannah—didn't come home last night after the party, and the Astons wanted to know if she's still at Coriston.' Shirley Morgan explained the details of the Astons' inquiries as retailed by Irene, and then added, ' I said we'd immediately investigate and make a thorough search and let her know, but to the best of our present knowledge, Hannah was not in the school—and certainly not in Browne's.'

'I see.'

'Do you? What do we say if we find that the damned girl spent the night snugged up with one of the prefects?'

'Better than if we find her body at the bottom of the swimming pool.'

Shirley Browne stared at her husband. But she accepted that this was no moment to have a lengthy discussion on the subject of Hannah Aston.

'Morgan, we've got to make inquiries and have a good look round, but let's be discreet as possible about it. You go over to School House and check it out. If necessary, get hold of the staff who live there, but don't involve the Headmaster yet. I'll snoop around Browne's, though I'd guess that, wherever Hannah's been, she's not here now. Let's hope and pray not. If something's happened to her, we don't want to be responsible.'

'All right.'

'And don't look as if the world was coming to an end. She'll turn up. Bad pennies do. It's probably a false alarm anyway. Her parents are inclined to flap.'

Morgan Browne nodded. He wasn't sure if Shirley was trying to encourage him or herself. It scarcely mattered. 'I'll meet you here or send you a message in forty minutes —or an hour at most. OK?'

'Yes. On second thoughts, Morgan, I suggest you try the san first. You never know.'

It was a sensible suggestion and Browne went straight there, to find Matron in her cubbyhole of an office. She was not in the best of tempers. She denied having seen Hannah Aston.

'Thank goodness!' she added. 'I've got enough on my hands at present. We're obviously in for a bout of flu. I've half a dozen down with it already. And to crown everything I was up at two in the morning coping with Ian Merger, who'd been sick all over his bed. I told Mr Condor after chapel that I suspected the boy had been drinking. His vomit stank of wine and—'

Browne made understanding noises and wondered how quickly he could get away. He was only half-listening. Ian Merger was not his problem. Hannah Aston was.

Leaving the san, he made a cursory search of the public part of School House. He glanced in the cloakrooms, where several coats were hanging, but didn't examine them. On a Sunday morning the whole building was quiet. On impulse he went over to the gym, which was empty. The door of the adjacent swimming pool was locked, as were the laboratories.

Morgan Browne then returned to his own house. Shirley was waiting for him, but she had nothing to contribute. While the girls had mostly agreed that it had been a good party and super fun, no one remembered Hannah in particular.

'What now, Shirley? I phone Mrs Aston?' Morgan said, trying to sound concerned but businesslike, his thoughts elsewhere. 'And depending on what she says—'

Irene Aston said little, but what she did say made unpleasant hearing; her daughter had been left in the care of Coriston College, more specifically in the care of Morgan Browne, and she was now missing. She assumed the Headmaster had been told. For her part, she proposed to call in the police.

CHAPTER 8

Detective Chief Inspector Dick Tansey studied his nails, which were well cared for. He could find no fault with them. Though he wouldn't have admitted it, even to himself, he was proud of his hands; like the rest of his body, they were long and thin. At last he raised his grey eyes and regarded his Chief Constable.

'You really want me to make it a priority to find this girl, Hannah Aston, who's been missing for less than forty-eight hours, sir?'

The response was the nearest to questioning an order that a Chief Inspector in the Thames Valley Police Serious Crime Squad could allow himself, and almost merited a rebuke, but Tansey was tired. He had just brought to a successful conclusion a long and complicated case involving a fellow police officer, which had caused him a lot of soul-searching. In comparison, this apparently trivial business of a missing schoolgirl didn't yet seem important enough to warrant the attention of himself or, indeed, of any officer in the Serious Crime Squad.

The Chief Constable shifted his large bulk in the chair that had been specially made for him. Fortunately Philip Midvale was both an astute and an understanding man. He appreciated that Tansey had had a hard time recently, which was one reason for giving him this relatively insignificant assignment. A second reason was more personal: the Headmaster of Coriston College, an old friend of Midvale's, had appealed to him directly in the hope that the mystery of Hannah's disappearance might be solved quickly and thus the school prevented from suffering unnecessary adverse publicity.

'Chief Inspector,' Midvale said slowly, 'no one will be better pleased than I if it turns out that the girl has run off to marry—or not marry—a boyfriend, or to seek her fortune in London, say. However, either theory raises two interesting questions. Why did she go at what must surely have been a most inconvenient time for her, late at night or in the early hours of the morning? And why did she go during a Hallowe'en party when she was dressed up as a witch? You might consider these points, Tansey.'

'Yes, sir,' said Tansey.

He had already thought of possible answers to the Chief Constable's questions but, knowing the man, he suspected that Midvale could have provided sensible explanations himself had he chosen to do so. No, it was clear that this was the Chief's method of signalling that the question of priorities was no longer a matter for discussion. It was to be Tansey's job to find Hannah Aston—and the sooner the better.

Tansey retired to his office and studied the information on Hannah provided by the few police officers stationed in Colombury when they had been called in by the Astons. There was very little, and he put it to one side in disgust. He thought for a moment and then sent for Bill Abbot. He had often worked with the extrovert sergeant, and knew how valuable could be his knowledge of the Cotswolds and its people; Abbot had been brought up in Colombury, as his soft Oxfordshire burr testified.

'Sergeant, we're off to your *alma mater*, if that's what we can call your home town of Colombury and, while we go, I want to hear all you can tell me about a school called Coriston College—which, I gather, is for some reason pronounced 'Corston'—and all about some people called Aston.'

Abbot grinned; he was used to Tansey. 'I'll do my best, sir. And you're right about Coriston being called Corston

—they're very particular on that point.' He embarked on his briefing.

Tansey listened carefully to what his sergeant was saying as they drove to Colombury. It was some years since Abbot, now married and with a family, had lived in the market town, but his parents were still there so he had kept in touch with the place. Tansey believed in detailed information and never despised gossip. However, as Abbot remarked, Colombury had grown considerably over the years, with more and more houses built on the outskirts, and he knew only the barest facts about the Aston family.

'It's a pity old Sergeant Court has retired,' Abbot said. 'He made it his business to find out as much as he could about all the newcomers to the district.'

Tansey hid a smile. He knew that the Astons would be considered 'newcomers' if they lived in Colombury for another twenty years, even in Abbot's eyes. But he too regretted the loss of Court, with whom he had worked on several occasions and who, in addition to his local knowledge, had the virtue of being prepared to seek help from Headquarters at Kidlington without unnecessary delay.

'Have you met Court's replacement?' Tansey asked.

'Sergeant Donaldson. No, sir. He's come from Reading and this is a promotion in rank for him. I'm told he's bit overkeen to prove himself.'

So he'll resent us being brought in over his head so soon, Tansey thought, and said, 'We'll make our number with him first, then go on to the Astons' and get some idea of this girl Hannah's family background. We've got to start somewhere.'

Sergeant Donaldson was a small straight-backed man with a military moustache, who looked as if he could never relax. He was punctilious in his attitude to Tansey who, in his mid-thirties, was two or three years his junior; Abbot he more or less ignored. They lingered at the police station only long enough for Donaldson to embroider his report with a few new details, and to learn what local steps had been taken.

'Not the sort of guy I'd enjoy having a pint with,' said Abbot in condemnation as he drove to the Astons' house.

'I doubt if we'll get a chance. He wasn't exactly hospitable,' said Tansey. 'Never even offered us a cup of coffee.'

'Would you say he treated the girl's disappearance rather lightly, sir?' Abbot inquired.

Tansey, who knew he had been guilty of the same attitude when he was discussing the case with the Chief Constable, hesitated. 'Donaldson's new,' he said. 'He's got a lot on his plate, settling in here. From what he told us he's done all that could be expected of him at this stage.'

'I wonder if the Astons would agree.'

'In cases like this, relatives are rarely satisfied,' Tansey said, regretting that Abbot had taken such an instant dislike to Donaldson. 'Of course we'll have to cover the same ground. You're slowing down, so this must be where we start—with Major and Mrs Aston. It seems they're expecting us.'

Indeed, forewarned by a telephone call from Kidlington, the Astons had been on the lookout for the police officers from Headquarters, and Richard came to the door to greet them. Although the officers had no means of comparison, anyone who knew him would have noted that he seemed to have become shrunken and defeated since Hannah's disappearance. Tansey introduced himself and Abbot, and Richard ushered them into the sitting-room where Irene faced them, fierce, angry and terrified.

Tansey was not surprised; he had seen such reactions many times before in personal crises. He asked one or two sympathetic questions, and then left the Astons to make the running. He noticed that Irene did most of the talking. Neither of them spoke in the least critically of their daughter.

Irene's criticisms were, in fact, reserved for the Eversleys and Morgan Browne. 'We thought we could depend on Bill Eversley, or Richard would have collected Hannah after the party himself. I shall never forgive Bill, never.'

'You think that Hannah, finding that the Eversleys had gone without her, set off home by herself?' Tansey asked.

'With great reluctance I've come to that conclusion, yes. What else can I believe, Chief Inspector? We've asked everyone with whom she might have gone. As for Coriston—evidently her Housemaster, Morgan Browne, just went off to bed and never bothered to check on any of his students. But the whole school's been searched now, all the buildings and the grounds, both by the staff and by some local police. She's not there.'

'It can only have been a cursory search. We'll have to have another one, with a proper team. Make a note, Abbot.'

'Sir.'

Tansey turned to Mrs Aston again. 'Would Hannah accept a lift from a stranger?' he asked.

'Not normally, no. She's a sensible girl.'

It occurred to Tansey that a sensible girl would have telephoned her parents or, if she thought they might be asleep, would have asked if she could spend the night at the College. Surely someone would have been available, even if not Mr Browne. To set off alone in the early hours to walk several miles through lonely lanes was asking for trouble. But he didn't voice his opinion.

'Is there any chance she might have left the party earlier, with a friend, perhaps?'

'Why should she, when it had been arranged she was to be brought home by the Eversleys?'

But there had been something evasive in Irene Aston's tone, and Tansey said, 'Does your daughter have a boy-friend, Mrs Aston?'

'No. She's a lot of friends of both sexes, but there's no one in particular.'

Mrs Aston sounded positive. Perhaps too positive, Tansey wondered, glancing at a large coloured photograph of Hannah that sat on a side table. The girl was almost seventeen, with beautiful hair and eyes. It was difficult to imagine that she was indifferent to admirers.

As if sensing Tansey's scepticism, Irene said, 'Hannah's a clever girl, and her chief interest at present is to do well at her school work. Isn't that so, Richard' she appealed to her husband.

'Yes indeed, dear.' Richard Aston seemed to wake from a reverie. 'Hannah was—is—' he corrected himself hurriedly, 'hoping to go up to Oxford in two years time, Chief Inspector.'

Abruptly Tansey changed the subject. 'We'd like to look at your daughter's room now, if we may, Mrs Aston.'

Tansey had risen to his feet, closely followed by Abbot, leaving Irene Aston little option but to accede to the request. With some reluctance she led the way upstairs to Hannah's room. She stood in the doorway, watching as the two officers made a fast professional search. She knew that she wanted to protest, though she couldn't say why.

It was Abbot who found the three snapshots taped to the back of an official photograph of the pupils of Coriston which the Sergeant had removed from its frame. It had been taken the first year Hannah was at the school. Tansey asked Irene if she could identify the snapshots and, lips compressed in an ill-concealed anger, she did as she was asked. They were all of Peter Merger.

'But these are old snaps, Chief Inspector,' she said. 'When we first came to Colombury Hannah went to the comprehensive school in the town as a temporary measure, and some of the students she became friendly with there were not—not altogether desirable. The Merger boy was one of them. However, when we decided to stay here, we sent her to Coriston where she's made much nicer friends. I expect she's forgotten about these old snaps of Peter.'

'Probably,' Tansey agreed. 'Does he still live in Colombury, this Merger boy?' He watched her hesitate; she wasn't a natural liar. 'If you don't know we can always—'

'Yes, yes, of course I know.' Irene spoke sharply, aware that she had betrayed her feelings. 'The Mergers run the off-licence in the High Street. It's a family business, and Peter went into it as soon as he left school.'

Tansey nodded his understanding. What a simple solution, he thought, if Hannah Aston had run off with Peter Merger. But when Abbot put this idea into words as they were driving away from the Astons' house, the Chief Inspector reminded himself and his sergeant that it was early days yet, and the inquiry had only just started. It was not a time to jump to conclusions.

While Irene and Richard fretted and fumed, dashed hopefully to answer the telephone, only to be asked more questions by the reporter on the local paper, and grew more and more short-tempered with each other, the two detectives had driven into Colombury. They left their car in the Mergers' car park and went into the shop.

There was only one customer, a big shambling fellow in his early twenties, who seemed to be having an argument with the man behind the counter. 'I want whisky, I told you,' he was saying. 'I've got the money. I earned it clearing up leaves in the churchyard for the parson. Why can't I have whisky?'

'Nick, it's not good for you. Take a couple of cans of beer

as you usually do.' The shopkeeper's patience was being tried.

He glanced at Tansey and Abbot. 'Yes? What can I do for you, sir?'

Tansey produced his warrant card. 'Chief Inspector Tansey of the Thames Valley Police, and this is Sergeant Abbot. I take it you're Mr Merger?'

'Yes. Alex Merger of Merger and Sons, wine and spirits merchants of Colombury.'

He grinned at his own announcement, showing perfect teeth, and Tansey thought that if Peter Merger was as good-looking as his father, it wasn't surprising that Hannah Aston should have been attracted to him. About to ask for Peter, Tansey was distracted by the customer who wanted whisky; he had suddenly bolted from the store, leaving the door open. Abbot went to shut it.

'Who was that?' Tansey asked.

'Nick Hayne. The poor lad's got a screw loose, but he's quite harmless.'

'Why did he bolt?' asked Abbot, who knew of Granny Hayne and Nick.

'Scared of the police at the moment. That new Sergeant Donaldson caught him urinating in the gutter in one of the back streets the other night and would have arrested him if his grandmother hadn't interfered.' Merger laughed. 'It takes a tough man to face up to Granny Hayne.'

'Then I hope I shan't have to,' said Tansey. 'Mr Merger, we'd like a word with your son, Peter.'

'He's away for a few days, Chief Inspector. Gone to London with a friend, to see a few shows and have some fun. He's been working hard and deserved a break.'

'Really? When did he go?'

'Saturday morning.' Merger's expression had become sardonic. 'And before you ask, I don't know where he's staying. He said they'd find somewhere quite easily. Nor did I bother to ask who was going with him. But I do know one thing. You can take my word for it that the friend isn't Hannah Aston.'

'Now why should you mention Hannah Aston, Mr Merger?'

'Oh, come on, Chief Inspector. Colombury's a small town. News travels fast here, and it's no secret that Hannah disappeared after a Hallowe'en party at Coriston on Saturday night. Add to that the presence of two important police officers from Oxford and the answer's not difficult.'

Tansey laughed. 'You're an intelligent man, Mr Merger, so I won't waste time. Is it right that Hannah and your son Peter were once—close friends?'

Merger pursed his lips. 'I'm not sure what you mean by close friends. Peter was desperately in love with Hannah once—puppy love, I suppose you'd call it, for he was only sixteen, and when she went to Coriston the friendship broke up. It might have survived. I believe Hannah was very fond of him, but they were only kids, and Mrs Aston did *not* approve. She didn't think Peter half good enough for her Hannah.'

'You didn't disapprove yourself?'

'No, why should I? As I say, they were only in their mid-teens, but you never know. I married my childhood sweetheart and it's been a great success. Why shouldn't Peter have done the same?' Suddenly Alex Merger grinned. 'Mind you, Chief Inspector, I'm not saying I'd have liked having Irene Aston in the family, as it were. The Major's OK, though he's none too prompt paying his bills, but his wife's no joy.'

'And Hannah?'

'A pleasant girl, friendly enough, but a bit withdrawn and nervous, like a horse can be nervous, if you know what I mean. It may seem a strange thing to say, but I got the impression that she wasn't a really happy child, and my wife thought the same.' Merger shook his head. 'It's not easy bringing up kids. I only hope the girl's come to no harm.'

'That was an interesting chat,' said Tansey as they went to collect their car. 'I'm beginning to feel I know Hannah Aston a little. Let's try the Eversleys now, Sergeant, and see if we can get to know her better.'

But at the Eversleys they were unlucky. The maid who answered the door said that Mr Eversley had gone to London for the day on business, and Mrs Eversley had taken the opportunity to go with him to do some early Christmas shopping. Miss Marjorie was at Coriston; she'd been upset by the disappearance of her friend, but Mrs Eversley had thought it best for her to go to school as usual.

'Where now, sir?' Abbot asked as, having thanked the maid, they once more returned to their car.

'The Windrush Arms,' said Tansey, looking at his watch. We'll have a pint and some lunch, and tackle Coriston College this afternoon.'

CHAPTER 9

'Morgan, where on earth have you been?' Shirley demanded sharply. 'Why didn't you come in to lunch? Stephen Blondel had to take your duty.'

Morgan Browne flung himself into his favourite armchair and regarded his wife bleakly. 'Was there any trouble? Stephen's not much good as a disciplinarian.'

'No. The news that Hannah Aston has disappeared has got around, and everyone's very subdued.'

'Good!' He nodded slowly. 'Let's hope that lasts.'

'Morgan, for Heaven's sake, what's happened?'

'Nothing yet, but soon everything's going to be disrupted. I've just been with the Headmaster. It seems he's been pulling strings with a chum of his—the Chief Constable of the Thames Valley Police. The end result is that this business of Hannah has been taken out of the hands of the local police. Two chaps from Headquarters, a Detective Chief Inspector Tansey and a Detective-Sergeant Abbot, are arriving this afternoon to make inquiries. They're going to report to him, and he's going to direct them to this House, asking them to make it the centre of their investigation. Sheringham's orders are that we're to give them every facility.'

'And what does that entail?'

'Not much to start with. A room where people can be interviewed—what I imagine they'll call an incident room, if the thing develops—and a runner—'

'A what?'

'A runner. Someone who'll dash off and winkle anyone the police want—staff or pupils—out of class to answer their questions. It won't be exactly conducive to work or discipline, will it?'

'Maybe not. But there's no point in being aggressive towards them, Morgan. The more we cooperate the sooner they'll go. I think I'll undertake this 'runner' role myself—at least I'll know where to find people.' Then a thought struck her. 'They're not sleeping here, are they?'

'No but they—or their minions—will be here for as long as it suits them. Probably over a period of days, even weeks. So it may be quite some while before we get rid of them.'

'Why should it? Hannah may turn up any minute—in London or Paris or anywhere. I know she was part of Browne's, but she was a day girl, Morgan. Her parents are surely ultimately responsible for her, not us.'

Morgan Browne got to his feet. 'You don't care a damn

about the girl, do you, Shirley? You don't care what may have happened to her. She may be dead, or—'

'And you seem to care too much, Morgan—much too much.'

They glared at each other, at the same time angry and frightened, both wishing they hadn't put their thoughts into such potentially accusatory words. Morgan was the first to recover, but he made no attempt to apologize.

'I've my scholarship class in a few minutes. Could you cope with these officers when they arrive, Shirley? I thought they might use one of the common rooms to start with; that would cause the least inconvenience to everyone. It'll be more comfortable than a classroom, and they'll have a telephone.'

'All right. I'll see to it,' Shirley said coldly. She wanted to cry.

'Perhaps we could start with you, Mrs Browne, if you don't mind,' said Tansey with a smile, after thanking her for the arrangements that had been made for their reception. He and Abbot had brought Sheringham a note of introduction from the Chief Constable, and the Headmaster had taken the opportunity to remind them once again of the need for a speedy resolution of the affair. Tansey had been politely non-committal.

He turned again to Mrs Browne. 'I'd guess you know as much as anyone about what goes on in this House, and probably in the school as a whole.' He waved her to a chair and sat himself behind the desk she had arranged to be brought into the room; Abbot sat to one side, unobtrusively ready to take notes. 'Tell me what sort of girl Hannah Aston is.'

'That's a broad question, Chief Inspector.'

Tansey registered that Shirley Browne was nervous, but he was not surprised; individuals were usually apprehensive when being interviewed by the police. 'I've seen a photograph of Hannah, so I know what she looks like. But was she studious, fond of music or games, for instance? Was she popular?'

'She was a clever girl. It was hoped she'd go up to Oxford. She'd lived in Germany—her father was in the Army—and she'd been well taught—except for Latin.' Shirley stopped abruptly, wondering what had induced her to mention Latin. 'But you're not interested in details like that.'

'Indeed I am, Mrs Browne. It all helps to build up a picture of the girl. What happened to her Latin?'

'Oh, my husband gave her special coaching, and she did quite well in the end,' Shirley said carelessly. 'It's that sort of school, Chief Inspector. She's concentrating on English, History and Modern Languages now, but she hopes to read English at Oxford, so Mr Blondel is giving her extra supervision.'

Shirley went on talking and Tansey listened. He was watching Mrs Browne, noting her hesitations, noting how she would mention a subject and then shy away from it. He was more interested in what she failed to say than in what she said. He sensed that she didn't like Hannah Aston, but was trying to hide her feelings.

'. . . and the last time I saw Hannah,' Shirley Browne concluded, 'was at about half past ten in the cloakroom during the party. I was mending Marjorie's dress, when Hannah came in to pin up her hair which had come loose.'

'Marjorie Eversley?'

'Yes. She and Hannah are close friends. Marjorie's not strong and she lives nearby, like Hannah, so her parents prefer her to be a day girl rather than a boarder. Chief Inspector, you asked if Hannah was popular. Well, the best I can say is that she wasn't unpopular, but there aren't many day students at Coriston, and the boarders do tend to form cliques.'

'Very natural,' said Tansey. 'Now, Mrs Browne, before we get on to the subject of the Hallowe'en party, one more question. Have you noticed any changes in Hannah recently?'

Shirley hesitated; she hadn't foreseen this question. 'Ye—es, you could say so, I suppose. She's not been working well this term. She doesn't seem to care whether she succeeds or not.'

'Do her teachers complain?'

'Yes. Mostly Stephen Blondel. He's her form master as well as her English teacher. My husband spoke to her about the complaints, but it seems it's difficult to get through to her. She appears indifferent to—to everything.'

There was the lightest tap on the door and Morgan Browne came in. He apologized for not having been there to welcome the police officers and explained about his scholarship class. 'I've four very hopeful boys,' he said with some pride.

Tansey congratulated him, and said that Mrs Browne had been the greatest help. He noted that the Brownes avoided looking at each other. 'Now that you're both here perhaps you'd tell me about this Hallowe'en party.'

'It sounds fun,' he said, when their concerted effort had come to an end. 'How recognizable was everyone—Hannah, for instance? Easily, because of her hair?'

'Her hair was hidden under a witch's hat that had straggly false hair attached to it,' Shirley said.

'But she was wearing the same outfit she'd worn for the last two years—a red skirt and white blouse with cabalistic signs on them,' her husband added.

Shirley's mouth set in anger as she tried to cover for what she thought of as a gaffe on the part of her husband. 'A lot of people keep to the same outfits,' she said. 'It's not easy to be original. There's always an abundance of ghosts and devils and—'

Sorry for her, Tansey interrupted, 'Could someone who was not connected with Coriston have put on some costume and joined the party?'

They stared at him blankly; it was clear that this idea had never occurred to either of them. 'Why should anyone do that?' Browne asked.

Tansey shrugged. 'To have a rendezvous with Hannah, perhaps?' He changed the subject again. 'It was a comparatively warm night, I'm told, but not one on which to linger outside. Am I right in thinking that once everyone had assembled in the main building for the party they wouldn't be likely to go outside again until they returned to their respective Houses?'

'Yes, that's right,' Shirley said at once.

Morgan shifted in his chair. 'As a matter of fact I did come back here,' he said. 'I had a sneezing fit and needed a handkerchief. And I stayed a while. I had a headache. The disco was very noisy."

Tansey thought this such a weak excuse that it had to be true. 'Did you see anyone while you were out?' he asked.

'No, I saw no one, either coming or going.'

'I think that's all for the moment, then,' Tansey said. 'Many thanks for your help. Could we see Marjorie Eversley next, please?' He waited until the Brownes were at the door before adding, 'Incidentally, I should warn you that a team will be coming from Kidlington tomorrow morning to conduct an extensive search of the College and its grounds. I hope the men won't cause too much disruption.'

'An interesting couple,' said Tansey when the Brownes had gone. 'Somewhat reticent and not altogether truthful, I fear, Abbot.'

'I got the impression, sir, that he was rather taken with Hannah Aston, but Mrs B wasn't so keen.'

'My impression too, Abbot. Let's hope we'll learn more on the subject from Marjorie.'

Perhaps Shirley Browne feared the same, for when she returned with Marjorie she sat down as if taking it for granted she should remain. She forestalled any comment from Tansey by remarking that she was not sure that one of the girl's parents shouldn't be there if she was being interviewed by the police. However, for the present she herself was prepared to act *in loco parentis*.

The Chief Inspector, who was naturally quite aware of the stringent regulations governing interviewing—or, more particularly, taking statements from—young persons, made no reply. And in fact, Marjorie clearly had no need of a chaperon or witness of any kind. She was only too eager to talk about Hannah.

'Oh, Chief Inspector, I couldn't bear it if anything's happened to her. I searched everywhere in School House I could think of after the party, and I asked some of the maids who were clearing up and the porter who was locking the doors, but no one had seen her. I was getting tired and Dad was getting impatient, and we decided she must have gone. But I do feel bad about it.'

'I'm sure you've no need to blame yourself,' said Tansey. 'You and your father kept to the arrangement you'd made. But let's go back to the beginning of the party. You and Hannah arrived together, I gather.'

'More or less.'

'What do you mean?'

'Well, Major Aston drove us both, but when we got here Hannah said I should go on ahead because she wanted to speak to her father—I've no idea what about—and we met up in the cloakroom a few minutes later.'

'What sort of mood was Hannah in?'

'She certainly wasn't enthusiastic about the party, but she's been down in the dumps lately and apt to be pretty short-tempered. I don't think she's too well, or she may be worried about something. She had a stupid accident the other day, and—'

'What sort of accident?'

Marjorie explained at some length about Hannah being thrown by Vain Glory at the Drivers' riding school. 'And she doesn't concentrate on what she's doing. Her mind seems to be somewhere else half the time. I did wonder if she was still upset about breaking up with Peter Merger, but she said not.'

'Peter Merger is not a pupil at Coriston,' Shirley Browne interjected quickly.

'I know, Mrs Browne,' said Tansey. 'Go on, Marjorie. Who else, apart from Peter, did Hannah particularly like?'

'Boys, you mean? It was more who liked her than the other way round, I think. Alan Carson—he's in Condor's House—was rather keen on her at one time. And I suspect Stanley Tranter too. He's Head of School and he and Hannah had the lead roles in last year's school play, opposite each other.' Suddenly Marjorie laughed. 'Then there's Mr Blondel.'

'Really, Marjorie!' Shirley Browne was angry. 'Gossip about the students is one thing, but to include the staff is —is—'

'I was only joking, Mrs Browne,' Marjorie persisted.

'And now you'll have to share the joke with us,' Tansey said smoothly.

'You tell them, Mrs Browne,' said Marjorie, who was not over-fond of Shirley Browne, though she respected Morgan.

'Tell them what?'

'Oh, about the paperchase, Mrs Browne—you know.'

'Very well, though it's completely irrelevant.' Shirley ignored Marjorie and addressed Tansey. 'Chief Inspector, at the beginning of the autumn term Browne's House always has a paperchase for staff and pupils. This year Mr Blondel and Hannah were the hares—not the most suitable pair, in my opinion. You'll be meeting Stephen Blondel, I'm sure; he's on our English teaching staff. Anyway, there was a sudden and violent storm in the middle of the run. The hounds abandoned the chase, but the two hares took shelter in a barn and Stephen twisted his ankle so they were very late back, and this led to a lot of silly sniggering. I must admit it was partly his fault. This is his first job, and he didn't deal with some of the puerile comments too kindly. But that's all there is to it.'

'Now if it had been Mr Driver, it might have been different.' Marjorie was not to be suppressed. 'Almost all the girls who know Rod are a little in love with him.'

'Marjorie, you really are a dreadful gossip!' Shirley's voice was sharp. 'Try to be sensible! This is a serious matter. Think of poor Hannah.'

'I do, Mrs Browne, I do. She's my closest friend.'

'And you've been a great help,' Tansey said. 'Mrs Browne, could you try to round up all the members of the staff who have been teaching Hannah this term? I think we'll start by dealing with them as a group.'

'Yes, I'll try to find them, though it may take a little time, because I'll have to arrange for temporary supervision. Fortunately Hannah's only taking four subjects at the moment, as I said, apart from extras like games and drama—and I teach the drama.'

'Right. Thank you, Mrs Browne.'

With a nod to Abbot, who had opened the door for her, Shirley Browne departed, propelling Marjorie in front of her.

'Poor woman,' said Tansey. 'She was terrified that Marjorie was going to suggest that her husband fancied Hannah.'

Abbot grinned. 'An interesting girl, Hannah, don't you agree, sir?'

'I do indeed, Sergeant. I wonder what this next lot will have to say about her.'

In the event none of them had a great deal to contribute. They all expressed concern. They all admitted that Hannah's work had deteriorated as the term progressed, that recently she had seemed tired and lackadaisical as if she didn't care, and that she could be insolent if reproached.

'Such a pity,' said Stephen Blondel. 'She's a clever girl, good university material.' And the others agreed.

'What about her as a person, apart from her work?' Tansey asked.

Here the accord was not so solid. The German Fräulein was effusive; Hannah was a dear sweet girl and it would be a tragedy if anything had happened to her. The two masters who taught History and French respectively said that they were not in Browne's House, and scarcely knew Hannah out of class; Mr Blondel would know her better. Stephen Blondel agreed that this was so, but pointed out that he had only been at Coriston for two terms, and Hannah was a day girl. 'Nevertheless, Mr Blondel, perhaps you'd be kind enough to stay behind for a moment,' Tansey said as Abbot, taking his cue, got up and opened the door for the other staff members.

Stephen Blondel peered at Tansey through his thick spectacles. He was obviously nervous, but doing his best to hide it. He hadn't liked being separated from his colleagues.

'You were Hannah's form master, Mr Blondel, and you taught her English, an important subject for her, I understand. You must have known her well, even if you've only been at Coriston for two terms.'

Blondel shrugged. 'It depends what you mean by well.

English was to be her scholarship subject and it was part of my job to give her extra coaching.'

'This is your first post. Hannah was not much younger than you. Did you think she was an attractive girl? You're not married, I take it?'

'No, Chief Inspector, I am not married. I don't even have a steady girlfriend, and you've been listening to gossip. That stupid hare-and-hounds race! There was a storm and we sheltered in a barn. For God's sake, we talked about English literature, but everyone seemed to believe, or pretended to believe, that we'd been—been—'

'Yes—how silly of them,' Tansey replied vaguely. 'I expect they were pulling your leg, Mr Blondel. A young schoolmaster's fair game, you know.'

'Not a very helpful bunch,' said Tansey when Abbot had ushered Blondel out. 'We may have to see one or two again, I guess. But enough for today. You've made a note of all the names they mentioned in relation to Hannah?'

Of course, sir, and there's a fair lot of them. They'll keep us busy tomorrow.'

Tansey stood up and stretched. 'Ah well. Sufficient unto the day. Let's go, Sergeant. If there's no word about the girl in the morning we'll have to start the wheels rolling—Headmaster and Chief Constable notwithstanding.'

CHAPTER 10

In November the sun does not rise early in the morning, but as soon as it was reasonably light a large van disgorged a group of police officers, men and women, outside Coriston College. They had come to give the school, and especially its grounds, a thorough search. It was considered that the

Houses and other buildings, which were in constant daily use, were unlikely to conceal Hannah Aston or yield much information, so at this stage they were regarded as of secondary importance.

Thus the exterior was to take priority, and the search would later include the road and lanes between the College and the Astons' house. The grounds and the area were large, and this effort would take far longer and be far more detailed than the preliminary search that had inevitably been hurried and cursory. An experienced officer from Kidlington, one Inspector Whitelaw, was in charge, but as a matter of routine Sergeant Donaldson of Colombury had been informed of the programme and was acting as his assistant.

Of course, everyone realized that the main object they were looking for was the body of a teenage girl, but nevertheless it had been impressed on the team when they were briefed that absolutely anything unexpected, or anything seemingly out of place, should be reported.

The Inspector, having obtained a plan of the College from the school secretary, who had been warned that one would be required by Tansey before he left the previous day, studied it and divided his party into groups. They set to work at once. Tansey had said that he would arrive later in the morning, when it was hoped that, with luck, something useful might have been found.

Fortunately there had been no rain since Saturday, but the search, as always, was to prove a long and tedious task.

Richard and Irene sat opposite each other at their kitchen table. They looked tired and depressed. Dr Fenwick had insisted that they should both take sedatives in order to get some rest, but the heavy drugged sleep had not given them a great deal of comfort.

At least their telephone was being monitored by the

police, so that it no long rang continually, and an officer stationed at the front door kept away unwelcome callers. But Richard and Irene knew that it was more than forty-eight hours since Hannah had gone to the Hallowe'en party, and still nothing had been heard of her.

Her photograph stared at Richard from the daily newspaper he was pretending to read, and her disappearance had been an item of news on television the evening before; the publicity didn't make life easier. My poor little girl, he thought bitterly, my poor little girl. Suddenly he was aware that Irene was speaking to him. He tried to smile at her.

'What, dear?'

'I said that I was going to sell poppies today, Richard. I promised I would, so I shall.'

'But how on earth can you, Irene? People will stop you in the street and inundate you with questions about Hannah. It'll be most unpleasant for you.'

'We can't hide ourselves for ever, Richard. Why should we? We've done nothing to be ashamed of, and nor has our Hannah.' Irene's voice broke. 'If she'd gone off of her own accord, I'm sure she'd have been in touch with us by now. She would know how worried we'd be and—and I'm certain she wouldn't let us suffer like this if she could help it.'

'No. I don't think she would,' Richard agreed sadly.

'But the alternative is hard to accept. Why our Hannah? I keep asking myself. Why not some other girl, who had brothers and sisters? Why take our only one?'

'Oh God, Irene, stop it! I can't bear it.'

Richard buried his face in his hands and his body shook, though no tears came. Irene stared at him with mild contempt. Apart from that one brief moment when she had broken down, they had been able to provide little emotional support for each other.

'Unfortunately we've got no choice. We can't just collapse, Richard. Hannah wouldn't want that.' Irene's voice was taut. 'So I shall go and sell poppies as planned. You'll be here if that Chief Inspector comes back, as he said he would. Presumably there'll be some news sooner or later.'

Richard lifted his head. 'Let's hope so.'

'Yes, it's this waiting that's so dreadful, not knowing, wondering . . . ' Irene didn't complete the sentence aloud, but she thought that if she knew that Hannah was dead she could bear it more easily, but wondering what might be happening to her at that very moment was soul-destroying. She told herself she must do her best to keep her mind on practical matters—selling poppies, for instance—or, in spite of what she had just said to Richard, she would collapse.

Alex and Rose Merger had finished breakfast. They too had been thinking of Hannah Aston and talking about her. Rose was adamant. The fact that Hannah had bought a half-bottle of gin from Peter on Monday of the previous week might or might not be relevant, but Chief Inspector Tansey should be informed.

'The trouble is your mind, Rose, my love.' Alex grinned. 'Anyway, Hannah told Peter it was to be a present for her dad's birthday.'

'Maybe that's what she told him, but it needn't have been true, Alex. You know as well as I do that when a girl wants to get rid of a baby one of the first things she'll try is gin—and a hot bath. It'll be easy enough for the Chief Inspector to discover if it was a present—and, if so, no harm done. But I'm sure he'll be interested to hear about it.'

'OK, Rose. I'll phone him now. He'll probably think me a fool, but anything for peace.'

Alex Merger was wrong, and his wife right; the Chief Inspector was interested. Anything connected with Hannah Aston interested him, and he wondered if there could be some truth behind Mrs Merger's suspicion. He asked Merger to thank his wife, and made a mental note to bear the possibility in mind.

'Mr Merger, it would be advisable if no one else learnt about this purchase of Hannah's. You understand?'

'Of course. You needn't worry, Chief Inspector. The wife and I like Hannah. We wouldn't start gossip about her.'

'Fine—and thanks again, Mr Merger,' Tansey said, and hoped for his parents' sake that Peter Merger was not involved in Hannah's disappearance.

As soon as Tansey had replaced his receiver, the phone rang again. He was told there was another call for him, from a Mrs William Eversley. When she was put through Mary Eversley was apologetic that she hadn't been in when he had visited the house the day before, but she would be in all this morning, and she wanted to speak to him. Tansey had intended to go straight from Headquarters to Coriston, but Mrs Eversley was persuasive.

'My daughter has been confiding in me, Chief Inspector, and you won't be wasting your time in coming to see her, I assure you.'

'I'll be there within an hour,' Tansey said, refusing to inquire what confidences Marjorie might have imparted.

And when the Chief Inspector and Detective-Sergeant Abbot arrived at the Eversleys' house they were received hospitably. The maid brought in coffee and biscuits at once.

'We thought that you had probably had an early breakfast, and would be glad of some coffee,' said Mrs Eversley, in explanation. 'I wouldn't let Marjorie go to school today, Chief Inspector. This business of Hannah is being a great strain on her, and she's not the strongest of girls. It seemed wisest to let her tell you what she wants to here with me, in her own home, rather than in front of Mrs Browne, kind though Mrs Browne is.'

'Quite,' said Tansey, realizing that Mary Eversley was one of those thin, elegant women with whom he never felt entirely at ease. He grinned at Marjorie. 'More gossip? It sometimes turns out to be very useful.'

'No, it's—it's not gossip. Hannah had a secret. I don't know what it was. She wouldn't tell me. But last Friday afternoon she cut classes. She said she had to go to Oxford, but she didn't want anyone to know, and would I cover for her.'

'And you did?' Tansey asked gently.

'Yes. Actually, it wasn't hard. It was only Fräulein, and then Mr Blondel, and Mrs Browne and reading for the school play. I said Hannah had a nose bleed. Fräulein didn't mind, but Mr Blondel looked at me oddly. I don't think he believed me. I'm not a very good liar. And Mrs Browne was annoyed about the reading. She said that if people weren't prepared to read for parts they couldn't expect to be in the play.'

'Do you think perhaps Hannah was meeting a boyfriend in Oxford, Chief Inspector?' Mary Eversley asked when Marjorie seemed to have nothing to add. 'It would be a simple explanation.'

'I've no idea,' Tansey said truthfully. 'Marjorie, would you say that Hannah was worried about something?'

'Yes. Yes, I would.' Marjorie was thoughtful. 'She was worried, but about all sorts of different things, actually. For instance, she used not to mind batty Nick Hayne, but the other day when I was with her she made us cross the road to avoid him.'

'You know about Nick Hayne, Chief Inspector?' Mary Eversley intervened. 'He's mentally defective, as they used to call it. Quite harmless, but something of a nuisance, and I suppose he could be frightening.'

'Not really, Mum.' Marjorie shook her head.

'Anyway, if someone did offer Hannah a lift on Saturday

night and abducted her, which I fear is the answer to Hannah's disappearance, I doubt if it was Nick Hayne. I'm pretty sure that he can't drive, Chief Inspector.'

'That would certainly seem to let him out,' Tansey agreed. 'And perhaps your fears will prove unjustified, Mrs Eversley. There's still a possibility that Hannah will be found alive and well.'

'Do you truly think so?' Marjorie asked eagerly.

'It's a possibility. No more than that.' Tansey said, and watched with regret as Marjorie's hopeful expression faded.

'Mrs Eversley was right. We haven't wasted time visiting her, have we, Abbot.'

'No, indeed, sir.' Abbot swung the car out of the Eversleys' drive and headed for Coriston. 'Excellent coffee and nice biscuits, at least.'

Tansey laughed. 'It all helps. But I was thinking of Miss Hannah's secret trip to Oxford the day before she disappeared. There must be some connection, however remote.'

'It may take some digging. She strikes me as being a secretive character.'

'Me too,' Tansey agreed, and fell into a brooding silence until they reached the College.

The big wrought-iron gates were shut, but there was a police officer on duty, and as they went up the drive there were more and more signs of police activity. The search of Coriston was well under way. Abbot, disregarding forbidding notices, parked in front of the steps of School House.

As they got out of the car Sergeant Donaldson came hurrying towards them. He was carrying a large plastic bag inside which could be seen a garment of some kind, blue in colour. He greeted Tansey and Abbot with surprising affability.

'I've just found Hannah Aston's coat, sir,' he announced

with obvious pride. 'And I've a witness to the fact that she was wearing the coat when she arrived for the Hallowe'en party. A Miss Monica Vaughan, the head girl of Browne's House or so she tells me, was in the cloakroom when Hannah came in that night.'

'Good,' said Tansey. 'Where did you find it, Sergeant?'

'Hanging on a peg in the girls' cloakroom, sir. I thought I would have a look around inside at the site of the party. The coat must have been there since Saturday, but the place is never really tidied up as girls are always coming and going.'

'I see,' said Tansey, ignoring Abbot's snort of disdain, and blaming himself for not having realized that Hannah would almost certainly have been wearing a coat over her witch's costume. 'Anything else?'

'Not at the moment.' Donaldson sounded disappointed that his discovery had not received more plaudits.

'Could you find Inspector Whitelaw for us, Sergeant? We'll wait for him in the car. There's no point in using the incident room until it's been properly equipped.'

'Yes, sir.'

Donaldson departed, and Tansey said, 'What do you make of the coat, Abbot?'

'It won't be much use to the forensic boys, sir, but at least it indicates that Hannah didn't leave Coriston of her own accord. It wasn't such a warm night that she'd have abandoned her coat. Doesn't look too good for her.'

'On the other hand it does suggest that she wasn't picked up by a stranger on her way home. It would seem to narrow the field of possible suspects, but I suppose we mustn't jump to conclusions.' Tansey was reflective.

'Here's the Inspector, sir,' Abbot interrupted.

'Right. I'll get in the back with him. Morning, Inspector. Any luck?'

''Morning, sir—Sergeant. Difficult to answer your question, sir, but we've found two or three interesting items, though they may well be irrelevant to the girl. You'll recall it rained hard on Friday morning, but it's been dry since then, so we can guess at approximate times for what evidence there is.'

Tansey nodded. 'Of course. That's a bit of luck, anyway. Go on, Inspector.'

'A vehicle—a car or a van—was parked in an open space at the edge of a belt of trees near the school's games pavilion. There are tyre marks and some small broken branches. It's not a very big space. I asked a games master who was organizing a rugger match if it was usual for anyone to park there, and he said it would be absolutely forbidden, and the vehicle can't have been there during daylight hours or he'd have seen it. That leaves Friday or Saturday night, and by the appearance of the leaves on the broken branches if I had to bet I'd favour Saturday.'

'Hm—m,' said Tansey. 'It would be quite a coincidence if there was no connection with Hannah. Interesting.'

'We also found a couple of bottles of wine and two glasses underneath the pavilion, sir. The glasses were cheap enough, but I know a bit about wine and these bottles were vintage claret—expensive stuff. Incidentally, they were too clean to have been there long—even under cover.'

'Well, I'm damned,' said Tansey. 'It might have been a midnight feast.'

'No sign of food,' said Whitelaw, grinning.

'As you know, sir,' Abbot said to Tansey, 'I'm a beer drinker myself, but isn't a bottle of wine per person a lot?'

Whitelaw answered. 'A fair amount, Sergeant, even during a dinner.'

'So we have a vehicle and two likely drunks. An original scenario,' Tansey said. 'I hardly dare ask what else you've got, Inspector.'

'Evidence that two people were making love in the

shrubbery on the other side of the playing field, sir.' The Inspector couldn't resist sounding pleased by this climactic announcement. 'There's no doubt. I've a man taking samples. It doesn't seem to have been a very satisfactory event. Perhaps it was interrupted.'

'Well, well!' said Chief Inspector Tansey, thinking with some satisfaction that Dr Sheringham, friend of the Chief Constable and Headmaster of Coriston College, was not going to welcome learning of the unofficial happenings at the school's Hallowe'en party. 'This is becoming a fascinating case. I only hope these various leads are going to help us trace Hannah Aston.'

CHAPTER 11

'Very well, if you must interrogate me, go ahead. I can't refuse to help the police, but be as quick as you can. I'm a busy woman. I've another two gone down with this 'flu, and I'm expecting Dr Fenwick any moment.' Matron was a forthright character, who spoke her mind. 'What do you want to know, Chief Inspector?'

'What can you tell me about Hannah Aston?' Tansey was equally businesslike

'Very little. She's a day girl, and I don't have much to do with her.'

'When did you last see her?'

'Early last week. She came to the san complaining of a sick headache. I must say I had my doubts about it. I thought she wanted an excuse to skip afternoon classes. She seemed very eager to get off home, and she recovered pretty quickly after a lie down and a couple of paracetamol.'

'When was this? Can you remember?'

'As it happens I can, and in any case it's entered in the

day book, like any other casualty. It was the Monday after she'd been thrown from her horse at the Drivers' riding school. Nothing to do with Coriston, of course, but I heard some of the boys talking about it. And, in fact, I discovered later that I'd maligned Hannah. She was really ill that night and her parents had to send for Dr Fenwick.'

At that moment a head came round the corner of the door and a hearty voice said, 'Entertaining, Matron? May I join you?'

'Yes. Come in, Dr Fenwick.' She introduced Tansey and Abbot. 'You can guess why they're here. Hannah Aston.'

Some of Dr Fenwick's ebullience left him and he frowned. 'A bad business!' he said. 'A bad business, indeed! The parents are very upset, naturally enough.'

'Matron tells me you'd been called to see Hannah one night before her disappearance,' Tansey said. 'What was the trouble?'

'Well, there's a question of medical ethics involved here, you know, Chief Inspector, but in fact the girl wasn't ill in the sense of having an illness, as far as I could see.' The doctor was hesitant. 'It was during the Monday night of last week. She had been vomiting violently for some while, and her mother was afraid she was becoming dehydrated. My examination suggested that Mrs Aston could easily have been right.'

'What did you diagnose?' Tansey asked.

'Nothing definite. A spot of food poisoning, perhaps.' Then, seeing Tansey's dubious expression, and afraid that he might have appeared to be too indifferent about a patient. 'I did examine her carefully and I prescribed plenty of liquids—sugar and salt, you know—and I phoned to ask after her on Wednesday, but she'd gone back to school.'

Tansey didn't altogether take to Dr Fenwick. He wished he could have been dealing with his old friend the senior partner, Dr Band. He decided to be blunt.

'Did you consider the possibility that she might have been suffering from the effect of alcohol or drugs?' he inquired.

'Er—yes.' Fenwick looked at the Chief Inspector as if Tansey had just read his mind.

'The idea did occur,' he went on after a moment. 'I—I thought her breath smelt of gin. But there was no point in upsetting everyone. If she'd been over-indulging she'd had a good sharp lesson, and I didn't want to make wild accusations.'

'She certainly hadn't been drinking when she came to me.' Matron was indignant. 'The Merger boy, the night of the Hallowe'en party—that was different. He was very drunk and he stank of wine. I told his Housemaster so.'

A bell rang; Matron was wanted in the sick bay. Hurriedly she departed, to be followed by Dr Fenwick as the police officers took the opportunity to leave. They had achieved more than they could have hoped.

'A nice sequence, sir,' remarked Abbot, without being asked. 'Monday, Hannah feigns sick, leaves Coriston early, buys gin. In the night she's violently ill, so ill that she has to spend Tuesday at home. Circumstantial evidence, of course, but it does support Mrs Merger's belief that the girl was pregnant and didn't like the idea.'

'It fits,' Tansey agreed. 'It definitely fits. I wonder if by any chance that's why she went to Oxford on Friday—to get advice from some kind of clinic.'

Abbot was surprisingly loquacious. 'What I can't understand is why she was in such a dither about her pregnancy. She's sixteen, almost seventeen, past the age of consent. OK! Perhaps marriage wasn't possible. The guy could be happily married. Or, more probably, she didn't want him as a husband. But there should have been no difficulty in getting an abortion. Why try this old wives' remedy? Why not tell her mother straight away?'

'I think it's the answer to your last question that's important, Abbot. Hannah couldn't bring herself to confide in her mother, not if it could be avoided. I don't know about you, but I can't imagine Mrs Aston being particularly sympathetic, or dealing with the problem very sensibly. I suspect she'd have made Hannah's life hell. She strikes me as the sort of woman who wouldn't believe it could happen to her daughter and would take it as a personal affront.'

'You mean it happens to "common" girls, but could never happen to her Hannah?' Abbot grinned. 'You may well be right, sir. Mrs Aston has a reputation for being a snob and, if the father turned out to be someone she felt unacceptable, she'd be doubly mortified.'

Tansey nodded his agreement. They were both thinking of Peter Merger, still presumed to be enjoying himself in London with a friend.

By chance, leaving School House, Tansey and Abbot met Shirley Browne and a tall girl with curly brown hair, who was introduced as Monica Vaughan.

'Just the people I wanted a word with,' Tansey said. 'I'm told the coat Hannah wore on Saturday night has been found in the cloakroom here.'

'Yes. I found it,' Monica volunteered. 'I knocked it off its peg by accident this morning and as I picked it up I remembered Hannah wearing it. I checked for a name tape, and found I was right. I gave the coat to Sergeant Donaldson. Is it important?'

'Maybe,' Tansey replied; Monica Vaughan's version of the incident was not identical to Donaldson's, but the Chief Inspector was prepared to believe it was nearer the truth. 'Thank you, anyway.'

He turned to Shirley, 'Mrs Browne, there are some boys we'd like to speak to—Alan Carson, Ian Merger and Stanley Tranter. Could you arrange it?'

'I expect so.' Shirley looked tired. 'If you go to the room we gave you for interviews at Browne's, Chief Inspector, I'll try to get hold of Mr Condor. They're all in his house.'

With renewed thanks Tansey and Abbot strolled off to Browne's House and the two women, having exchanged smiles, went their separate ways, Shirley Browne to find Lance Condor and Monica to her mathematics class.

Abbot said, 'Did you notice how Monica Vaughan reacted to the name of Stanley Tranter, sir? Her eyes widened and she seemed disturbed. I'd guess she doesn't quite like the idea of us talking to Stanley.'

'No, I didn't notice that. Good for you, Abbot. We'll have to see how Mr Tranter reacts to Miss Vaughan's name.'

But for this they had to wait. Condor, a tall, thin man who resembled a stork, arrived with Alan Carson and Ian Merger and said someone was fetching Tranter. Ian was asked to wait outside while Alan was interviewed, with his Housemaster in attendance.

'I believe you were a friend of Hannah Aston's,' Tansey began.

'Then you believe wrong, Chief Inspector. I meet her at the riding school, but she's a poor horsewoman. That accident she had—I'm sure you've heard about it—was completely her fault. She was just showing off in front of Mr Driver, which was typical of her.'

'You didn't like her?'

'Not overmuch. I'm in the same set for English as she is, and she plays up to the master—Mr Blondel, taking up his time—which is annoying for those of us who want his attention too.'

It seemed to Tansey that Alan Carson was too vehement in his dislike of Hannah, but he didn't press the point. And, after a few more questions, he let the boy go.

Then, Alan dismissed, Ian Merger came in. On the surface Ian, in appearance a young version of his father, was polite and innocent, surprised that the officers should want to talk to him at all. Tansey didn't dislike the boy, but at once distrusted him. Ian assured him that he knew nothing of bottles of wine under the games pavilion. Matron was mistaken; he had been suffering from food poisoning on Saturday night—something he'd eaten at the Hallowe'en party—and if they were thinking he could have taken wine from his father's shop they were also mistaken. In such a business a very careful inventory of stock was maintained. It was a convincing performance.

Lance Condor spoilt it. He had been listening with a mixture of boredom and irritation; his time was being wasted when he should have been teaching. But as Ian Merger continued to swear innocence and ignorance a slow smile irradiated his sharp pointed features.

'Stop telling lies, Ian,' he said suddenly.

'Lies, sir?' Ian was shocked. 'You can ask my father.'

'No need. I know where that wine came from—Brigadier Carson's cellar—and you and Alan got drunk on it together when you should have been at the Hallowe'en disco.'

'Sir,' Ian said weakly.

'Now, start again,' Condor said. 'I doubt if these police officers are interested in your drunken debauchery. You and Alan can see me about that in my study at six this evening. Meanwhile, try answering the Chief Inspector's questions truthfully.'

'Yes, sir.' Ian looked doubtfully at Tansey.

'Mr Condor's right, Ian,' Tansey said. 'I'm not in the least interested in your drinking. What I want to know is did you or Alan see anybody while you were in the grounds?'

'A car was parked among the trees near the pavilion, sir. It drove off across the playing field as we got there, nearly knocked us down, it did. It didn't have its lights on, but the moon came out and we saw it clearly. It was an old Ford and—and we both agreed that Major Aston was driving it, sir.'

Tansey hid his surprise. 'Have you any idea what time this was?'

Ian shrugged. 'Between half nine and ten, sir.'

'Anyone else?'

'I didn't see anyone else, but Alan swears that as we were going back to School House he saw a ghost, all white and ten feet tall, he said. Personally, I think he dreamt it. We weren't exactly sober by then, sir.'

'I'm not surprised,' Tansey said drily and gave his sergeant a reproachful glance as Abbot turned a snort of laughter into a cough. 'Off you go then, Ian, and thanks for your help.'

'In fact, it's you I should thank, Mr Condor,' Tansey added when the door had shut behind Ian. 'How on earth did you know?'

'Well, I hadn't paid much attention to Matron when she told me that Ian had been drunk that night. But I got a letter from Brigadier Carson this morning complaining that Alan was tight when Carson's chauffeur picked him up after the party; the boy often goes home for a day or so at weekends. Then you provided the final clue and the rest, Chief Inspector, was simple deduction.'

Tansey grinned but, before he could make any comment, there was a perfunctory tap at the door and Stanley Tranter came in.

'You wanted me, sir?' he said, addressing Condor and ignoring the police officers.

'This is Stanley Tranter, our Head of School,' said Condor with a certain amount of irony. 'Detective Chief Inspector Tansey and Detective-Sergeant Abbot. Sit down, Stanley.'

Stanley Tranter sat and crossed his legs, making it plain

that he was at ease. 'I assume this is about Hannah Aston,' he said.

'You assume right. What was your opinion of her?' Tansey said.

'I scarcely knew her, but she struck me as being a rather arrogant girl—the *noli me tangere* type.'

'The *what*?'

Stanley smiled patronizingly. 'In vulgar parlance, Chief Inspector, not a girl who was likely to enjoy a little slap and tickle.'

'Or a roll in the shrubbery on a dark night?'

There was a silence. The colour had drained from Stanley Tranter's face. He stared at Tansey in disbelief. Then he must have told himself that the Chief Inspector couldn't possibly know

'That sounds uncomfortable,' he said, his voice steady.

'Probably. Tell me, at your Hallowe'en party did you notice Hannah—dance with her, perhaps?'

Tranter relaxed. 'I didn't dance with her, but I remember noticing her once. I banged into her by mistake. She was with another devil.'

'Another devil?'

'There were a lot, as usual. Quite a few of the male staff go as devils. All you need to do is stick a tail on your dinner jacket and wear some kind of headgear with horns. Simple.'

'And simple to get it cleaned if anything was spilt on it. Which reminds me,' Tansey said absently. 'Sergeant, make a note that we must speak to Monica Vaughan again, will you?'

'Sir!'

Tansey turned back to Stanley Tranter, who was again several shades paler. 'I'm sure you know that detective work is largely composed of amassing bits of information, much of which turns out to be quite irrelevant. Now, at the moment we're interested in anyone seen in the grounds of

Coriston on Hallowe'en, especially after nine-thirty and in costume or otherwise. It could even be an intruder, and not a member of the College. So if you hear of anything, however seemingly trivial, that might help, please let me know. After all, as Head of School, you're probably in a better position to pick up unconsidered trifles than I or a member of staff.'

'Yes. I'll do what I can—sir.' Stanley Tranter spoke through his teeth. 'Anything else?'

'No. You can go. Thank you for your assistance.'

When Tranter had departed, Lance Condor asked, 'Was all that of any use, Chief Inspector?'

'Bread on the water, I hope, Mr Condor.' Tansey sounded cheerful. He had chanced his luck, and the ploy had come off. What's more he had put that supercilious young man in his place. Whether it would prove any help towards finding Hannah was another matter.

Condor stared at the Chief Inspector doubtfully. 'You've talked to the boys you asked for, so is there anything else I can do? If not, I'll be off to my abandoned flock to see what mischief they've been up to in my absence.'

'Nothing else for the moment, Mr Condor. We'll be off ourselves after we've checked with the team searching the place. Many thanks for your help and support.'

'Off where, sir?' Abbot asked fifteen minutes later as he and Tansey got into their car.

Inspector Whitelaw had had nothing further to report. His team would be taking a break and then would be continuing their search of the land on either side of the road and lanes leading to the Astons' house. He would make a final report on his return to Headquarters, where it would be decided if the search should be extended the next day.

'The Windrush Arms, Sergeant. We'll have a pint and a sandwich, then pay this riding school a visit.'

CHAPTER 12

'Another week at least,' said Audrey Driver in disgust as the vet drove off. 'How can we rest Glory for another week? It means either working the other good horses too hard, or putting decent riders up on duds.'

'We don't have any choice.' Rodney was sombre. 'We're insured against pupils falling off or getting injured, of course, but it's never occurred to us to insure against injury to the horses. I suppose it should have done.'

Abruptly he stopped speaking. A car had driven into the yard and two men got out—Chief Inspector Tansey and Sergeant Abbot, not immediately recognizable as police officers, but carrying with them an air of officialdom.

'Who the hell are they?' Rodney murmured.

'Trouble, I expect.' Audrey sighed. She was not by nature a pessimist, but recently the Driver enterprise seemed to be out of luck and going through a bad patch. 'Good afternoon,' she said as she went forward to greet Tansey and Abbot.

'Good afternoon.' Tansey introduced himself and his sergeant. 'Sorry to bother you, but we'd like to ask a few questions about Hannah Aston. Get a different perspective on her, as it were—different from her family and school, I mean.'

The Drivers exchanged glances, and Audrey said, 'We were just speaking of her—indirectly. Come along in.'

Audrey told the story of Hannah's accident succinctly, though she failed to conceal a certain amount of bitterness. 'I think she lost her temper and hit the horse when it failed to do what she asked of it. Luckily she wasn't badly hurt, only shocked a little, but the Astons made a great fuss.'

'It was really my fault,' Rodney said. 'I shouldn't have let Hannah ride Vain Glory. She wasn't up to it, though she flattered herself she was. And it's landed us in a hell of a mess.'

Audrey explained the consequences of Vain Glory's injury. 'We work hard. We have to, in order to keep this place going, and at present with the recession it's touch and go if we'll survive. But there's a limit to what we can get out of the horses.'

Tansey nodded his sympathy. Then he added, 'I take it you've not seen Hannah since this episode.'

'Yes, I have,' they said together, and stared at each other in surprise. 'When?' they began, and laughed as Audrey said, 'OK, you first, Rod.'

'I saw her on Monday, in Colombury, outside Mergers' off-licence. I suggested she might persuade her mother to let her continue her riding lessons, but the little madam spurned the idea.'

'You didn't like Hannah much?'

'If you want to know, I thought she was an arrogant, conceited girl, but the Astons paid, though sometimes they were pretty slow about it.'

Tansey noted that Driver's answer had been similar to Alan Carson's.

'And you, Mrs Driver, when did you last see Hannah?'

'On Friday afternoon, in Oxford. She was with Morgan Browne, her Housemaster. I saw them go into a tea-shop in Ship Street together. They didn't see me and I've not mentioned it to anyone. I don't like to start gossip, Chief Inspector.'

'You're quite sure of this, Mrs Driver.'

'Quite sure.'

'Right.' Tansey slid into his next question. 'That was on

Friday. Saturday was the night of the Hallowe'en party at Coriston. Were you both at home?'

'I was. Audrey wasn't.'

'I went over to Chipping Norton to see my mother, who lives there,' Audrey explained. 'I got home about twelve. The trip meant I drove past Coriston twice, but I didn't see anything untowards, except for the fairy lights in the drive.'

'And you were at home alone, Mr Driver.'

'Yes, as I said.' And after a slight pause Rodney added. 'I checked on the horses, especially Vain Glory, around eleven, but I didn't leave the premises. I didn't go and haunt Coriston, Chief Inspector—even on Hallowe'en.'

Tansey laughed, but he registered the fact that Rodney Driver was not a stupid man—and he had disliked Hannah. Why? Just because of her so-called arrogance and conceit? Or was there another reason? He recalled Marjorie Eversley's comment that almost all the girls who rode were a little in love with their good-looking riding master, and he wondered if Driver's vanity had been wounded by Hannah's refusal to comply, to flirt mildly with him as the others did. Hannah, he thought, was an unusual girl.

'That's fine then,' he said. 'We'll be on our way.'

After their visit to the Drivers' establishment, the two police officers separated. Sergeant Abbot, at Tansey's request, went to pay an unexpected call on his mother in the hope of gleaning any local gossip that might be relevant to Hannah's disappearance. The Chief Inspector drove on to the Astons'. He had some queries in mind and he thought he might be more likely to get truthful answers if he were alone.

He discovered that Irene had gone out. To sell poppies, the constable on duty in front of the house told him, expressing some amazement at her audacity—a view that Tansey shared. And the Major had a visitor, the Reverend William Weston, doubtless come to offer moral support.

'No news,' Tansey said. 'I'll let you know as soon as there is, Major Aston, I assure you.' He wished the vicar would go.

'This waiting and not knowing is such a strain on the family,' said Weston.

It was a platitude, but none the less true. Tansey thought that Richard Aston looked in deplorable shape. He had shaved badly, nicking himself in a couple of places. His skin was sallow, his clothes dishevelled, his shoulders bowed and he had a general air of discouragement.

'. . . such a clever, intelligent girl,' the vicar was saying. 'And a happy girl, with everything to live for. My dear Richard,' he hurried on, 'we're all praying for her, and for you and Irene.'

'Thank you,' Richard Aston replied. 'I'll tell Irene.'

The vicar got to his feet and, presumably merely to make further conversation, said, 'I saw the elder Merger boy—the one who Hannah used to be friendly with—over at Shipton last Sunday. It was a surprise to see him there. I don't know what he was doing. The usual priest at St Cuthbert's was ill and I was asked to take Matins for him.'

'You work too hard, William,' Richard said, uninterested.

Tansey, on the contrary, was very interested. What was Peter Merger doing in Shipton, half an hour's drive from Coriston College, when according to his father he was meant to be enjoying himself in London? But it was a question that would have to wait. William Weston was taking his leave.

On his return from seeing the vicar to the door Richard Aston said, 'What is it you want, Chief Inspector? Not more questions, I hope.'

'I'm afraid so, Major Aston. Please bear with me.' Tansey sounded considerably less assertive than he felt. 'On Saturday night when you got to Coriston, Marjorie tells me she went ahead into School House because Hannah said she wanted to speak to you alone. What about?'

'I—I—' Richard Aston stuttered. He was tempted to say he couldn't remember, but realized that this would be an obvious untruth. He tried to think quickly. 'A Christmas present for Irene—her mother. Yes, that was it. She wanted to ask me what Irene would like.'

'Not a terribly urgent question at the end of October, surely?' Tansey pressed home his advantage. 'And yet you didn't drive home at once, Major. You parked in the College grounds near the games pavilion, and thought about your conversation with Hannah for a very long time. Or were you thinking of something else?'

'How—Oh, I suppose those two boys recognized my car or me. I knew I shouldn't have parked there, but I wasn't —wasn't feeling well.'

'You mean you were upset, worried, because of what your daughter had just told you—that she was pregnant?'

Richard Aston recoiled as if Tansey had struck him. He didn't ask how Tansey knew; in fact, it was an inspired guess on the part of the Chief Inspector. Aston nodded, dumbly. He seemed unable to speak. At last in a low gruff voice he said, 'I couldn't believe it at first, but she assured me there was no doubt though she hadn't had a test. She'd missed her period for two months. She said that whatever happened Irene must not know, and I must help. She couldn't—wouldn't—have the baby.'

'Did she tell you who the father was?'

'All she would say was that there had been no one else but—him, and she must have an abortion, which would take a lot of money. She'd made inquiries. She kept on repeating that her mother mustn't know and I must help her, but she remained very calm. She was much calmer than I was, in fact. She said I must think what was to be done.'

'Did you agree to help her?'

'Of course I did! How could I refuse? I loved—love—her. But the absurd point was that once I'd got over the shock I was forced to face the fact that I couldn't think how I was going to help her. There was the money and the arrangements. The clinic would want her to stay overnight. I'd no idea how to organize all this without Irene knowing. We're a very close family.'

'Why was it so important your wife shouldn't be told?'

'Dear God! You ask that? Because—Chief Inspector, you don't know Irene. She's set her heart on Hannah achieving all the things she hoped to achieve herself, but has failed to do because I haven't been a—a satisfactory husband. Anyway, it doesn't matter now, does it? I can only hope and pray that Hannah decided I'd be inadequate and has gone off on her own—and, when it's done, she'll get in touch.'

The Chief Inspector thought of the coat left hanging up in the cloakroom, and now on its way to the forensic laboratory. Even if Hannah had run away on the spur of the moment—and the decision would have to have been made in the middle of the disco—she wouldn't have abandoned her coat, which would have provided cover for her witch's costume. More likely she would have left the hat with its attached grey locks, but this had not been found. And what about money?

Tansey couldn't accept this as a credible picture of events. If Hannah, in a moment of despair, had gone off on her own, it was clear she hadn't been prepared to go far. It was more likely she had intended to kill herself, but how had she planned to do this, and where was the body? No, everything pointed to the involvement of someone else.

The rattle of a key in the lock of the front door brought the Chief Inspector and Major Aston back to the present.

'That'll be Irene,' Aston said. 'For God's sake, don't tell her, Chief Inspector. I beseech you. I promised Hannah her mother would never know.'

'All right.' Tansey found himself unable to refuse.

Irene Aston came into the sitting-room. 'Ah, Chief Inspector, I saw your car outside and the officer said you were here. Any—any news?'

'Not yet, I regret to say, Mrs Aston.'

'How did the poppy-selling go, dear?' Richard made a great effort to appear normal.

'Not too bad. Everyone was very kind, too kind in fact. It's not pleasant to be an object of pity.' Irene looked inquiringly at Tansey. 'Is there any special reason for your visit, Chief Inspector?'

'I've been trying to trace Hannah's movements during the week leading up to her disappearance,' Tansey said with some truth. 'It seems to have been an unfortunate week, what with accident and sickness. Tell me about Friday. She was late home?'

'Yes. Mrs Browne should be more considerate than to keep the day girls late in the winter, but she's very keen on this play of hers, and of course last year Hannah had an important part. At least Mr Blondel brought her home.'

Blondel? Stephen Blondel, Hannah's English teacher? Someone was lying, Tansey thought. Marjorie said Hannah had planned to go to Oxford on Friday afternoon. Audrey Driver said she had seen Hannah with Morgan Browne, Hannah's Housemaster, go into a café in Oxford on Friday afternoon. But now . . . Before he could frame a tactful question, Mrs Aston had more or less answered it.

'I told her she should have invited him in for a drink, but she said he had an appointment which is why she'd asked him to drop her at the end of the lane.'

So it was probably Hannah who had lied. Tansey was not surprised. Some unfortunate detective-constable, equipped with the girl's photograph, would have to plod around Oxford tracing her movements. That shouldn't prove too difficult.

And then? Talks with Morgan Browne and Peter Merger, more interviews, an extension of the search? And of course Hannah Aston would turn up, minus her unborn child and, while the public complained of the increase in burglaries and car thefts and assaults and mindless vandalism, days of police time would have been wasted.

But there were still the problems posed by the coat left hanging on a peg in the cloakroom to be explained, and Hannah's choice of going away clothes.

Thankfully the Chief Inspector said goodbye to the Astons and set off to met Abbot in the Windrush Arms.

Bill Abbot had spent an enjoyable couple of hours with his parents, but he had learnt little that was relevant to the inquiry into Hannah Aston's disappearance. The general opinion in Colombury seemed to be that Hannah had eloped, probably with Peter Merger who was known to be away from home, or that on leaving Coriston after the Hallowe'en party she had been pulled into a stranger's car, and her body would be found weeks or months later, probably many miles away. There were, of course, variations on these two themes; a great deal depended on how much sympathy was felt for Richard and Irene Aston.

'Another suggestion Dad heard, sir,' said Abbot, 'was that Nick Hayne was responsible, and that's already caused trouble. Some boys started teasing him about it last night, saying he'd drowned the girl in the old quarry up Shipton way, and he went for them and knocked a few of their teeth out. He's got a temper, has that lad.'

'Where is he now?'

'Out on bail. Incidentally, sir, Mrs Eversley was wrong when she said she believed Nick couldn't drive. He may not have a licence but he knows how. Last summer he worked as a parking attendant, and he must have had to move cars around then.'

'We'll have to look into him, I suppose.' Tansey sighed. 'But not this afternoon, Sergeant. We've done enough for today. There'll be a pile of paperwork waiting when we get back to HQ, and it'll take me a good hour to prepare tomorrow's report for the Chief Constable. Nick Hayne will have to wait.'

'Yes, sir,' said Abbot, pleased at the thought of getting home to his wife and child at a reasonable hour.

CHAPTER 13

'We're to pull out all the stops. The search for Hannah Aston is to be intensified and widened immediately—Chief Constable's orders,' Tansey said,

'For her or her body?' Whitelaw asked sombrely.

The Inspector and Sergeant Abbot were in Tansey's office. Tansey had just returned from reporting to a senior officers' conference, including the Chief Constable and the Chief Superintendent in charge of the Serious Crime Squad.

'Both,' Tansey said. 'We're to treat it as a potential murder case. I'm holding a press conference at ten this morning. The idea is to get as much publicity as possible through the media in the hope of tracing her if she's alive. The Chief Constable called Dr Sheringham, who agreed reluctantly. He really had no alternative. It won't do Coriston College any good, but the girl's got to come first. Fortunately her long corn-coloured hair is so distinctive that if anyone saw her that night they'll probably remember, especially if she was still wearing part of that witch's costume . . .'

'And if she's dead, which in my opinion is the more likely,' said Whitelaw, who was a practical man, not over-imaginative. 'Extend yesterday's search, you said?'

'That's your job, Inspector.'

'It's going to take a lot of manpower.' Whitelaw was not happy at the prospect. 'The country around that part of Oxfordshire is heavily wooded.'

'The manpower will be made available,' said Tansey.

Whitelaw turned to Abbot. 'Sergeant, you're a local. If you were going to bury a body in a place not far from Coriston, where would you choose?'

'Any wooded copse, sir,' said Abbot after a moment's thought. 'Somewhere not close to a building where I might disturb a dog, say, but near a road so as not to have to carry the body further than necessary.'

'All that sounds pretty sensible.' Whitelaw nodded his agreement.

'But actually I wouldn't try to bury it at all, sir,' Abbot continued. He was enjoying his unusual position as a consultant and adviser to his seniors. 'Certainly not at this time of year when the ground's hard, not unless I was in no hurry and could make a leisurely job of it.'

'So what would you do with it?'

'I think I'd throw it into the old disused quarry up Shipton way. The quarry's fenced, but the fence is broken down in places and a whole pile of junk has been chucked in there. It's become a kind of unofficial rubbish dump. People complain about it regularly but nothing gets done.'

Tansey objected. 'But if it's a popular place to dump stuff wouldn't someone notice a body down there?'

Abbot shook his head. 'It's not that kind of quarry, sir. It's full of water, has been for years.'

Whitelaw groaned. 'Don't tell me we're going to have to drain the damned place?'

'I don't think that would be possible, sir. I'd guess that divers are the only answer.'

'Won't the body float to the surface after a few days—if it's there and assuming it's not been weighted?' Tansey suggested.

'It might, sir, but on the other hand it might not. There's so much rubbish lying about on the bottom that it could easily get entangled.'

Tansey pictured Hannah's beautiful hair wrapped around some rusting metal object, her once trim body slowly swelling with gases. Although he had never met the girl, it was not a pleasant thought.

He was thankful when the practical Inspector Whitelaw distracted him.

'There's no chance of organizing divers today,' said Whitelaw. 'It takes time to do that, as you know. So I suggest I get my men going on the woods and the roadside ditches. If we find nothing I'll lay on divers tomorrow for first light on Friday. Is that OK, Chief Inspector?'

'Sure,' Tansey agreed and, to encourage Abbot, added, 'But you might get a good man to have a look round the edge of this quarry.'

'Will do,' Whitelaw promised.

'Meanwhile I'll do my best to inspire the media. Then you and I will be off to Colombury again, Sergeant.'

'Yes, sir. I'll have the car ready.'

In the event, however, there was to be a delay. After his well-attended press conference, the results of which were fully satisfactory, Tansey found that Peter Merger had arrived, unbidden, at Headquarters, and was asking to speak to him.

*

'I got home this morning, Chief Inspector, and Dad said you wanted to see me. It'll be about Hannah Aston, I presume.'

'That's right.'

Tansey studied the dark, good-looking young man who sat across the desk from him, and thought that Peter Merger did indeed take after his father, and not only in appearance. Peter seemed to possess all Alex Merger's frankness and charm. It wasn't surprising that Hannah had found him attractive.

'I'll do anything I can to help,' Peter said. 'I was very fond of Hannah once.'

'So I gathered,' said Tansey drily. 'Well, let's start with the gin.'

'Ah yes, *mea culpa*. I sold her a half bottle. She said it was to be a birthday present for her old man. She paid cash for it. I found a plain bag at her request, and she went.'

'And that was the last time you saw her?'

'No! Scarcely had she gone than she came back into the shop.' Peter recounted Hannah's apprehension on seeing Nick Hayne inspecting her bicycle. 'Silly of her, as I said. Nick's perfectly harmless unless someone deliberately riles him. He'd never hurt Hannah. Anyway, that was on Monday. Then I saw her again on Friday. That was the last time.'

'Friday?'

'Yes. I'd been into Oxford on a job for Dad, and on my way home I was flagged down by Mr Browne of Coriston. His car . . .' Peter explained what had happened, then went on, 'Anyway, I dropped Mr Browne off at the garage as he asked, and drove Hannah to the bottom of the lane near her house. She didn't want the Mergers' van driving up to the front door. I quite understood why—Mrs Aston never made any secret of her disapproval of me.'

'Did you ask Hannah what she'd been doing in Oxford?'

'Yes. She told me to mind my own business.'

'What about Saturday?' Tansey was casual.

'What about it? I never saw Hannah on Saturday. As I said, Friday was the last time I set eyes on her.'

'Your father told me you went to London with a friend on Saturday.'

'So?' Peter had become wary.

'That wasn't exactly true, was it? You were seen in Shipton on Sunday morning, Mr Merger, not far from Coriston.'

'Possibly, Chief Inspector. But my father didn't lie. He told you what he believed to be the truth. I set off to go to London, intending to pick up my girlfriend on the way, but when I got to Shipton where she lives she said she couldn't leave her mother, who was unwell. We decided to wait twenty-four hours and hope we might be able to go then, which is exactly what happened. We went to London on Sunday after an early lunch.'

'You spent Saturday night in your girlfriend's house. Her parents will vouch for you?'

'There's only her mother, and she'll vouch that I was there, yes, but—I didn't sleep in the house. It's very small, only two bedrooms. Mrs Fanshawe sleeps in one, and my girlfriend shares the other with her young sister.'

'But couldn't you have slept downstairs on the floor—or on a sofa?'

'No, not really. Mrs Fanshawe's a worrying sort of woman. It would have bothered her. I told her I was going home. In fact, I spent the night in my Fiat at the edge of the woods. But if you think, Chief Inspector, that I had anything at all to do with Hannah's disappearance, then you're wrong.'

Their eyes met. They challenged each other. Peter was the first to look away.

He stared out of Tansey's office window. 'We were only kids,' he said quietly, 'Hannah and me—but I loved her,

I really did. No one will ever be quite like Hannah as far as I'm concerned. And yet we never did more than kiss and fondle each other a little. Hannah was not exactly cold, but —I doubt if I'd put up with it now. Then, it was all she wanted, and I accepted.'

'I think I understand,' said Tansey gently. 'You've spoken to your parents—your mother?' He was in no doubt that Peter Merger had been in love with Hannah, or had thought he was; but people sometimes kill those they love, especially if they can't possess the object of that love. But the lapse of time between the end of their relationship, if it could be called that, and the murder, if there had been one. If . . . If . . . Tansey thought.

He said, 'Did it surprise you to learn that Hannah might be pregnant?'

It was a full minute before Peter Merger answered, and when he did speak his words were carefully chosen. 'If that's true, Chief Inspector, and I assume it is, then I'm sure it wasn't the result of some casual—happening. She must have loved the man very much. She was a fastidious girl—old-fashioned if you like—at any rate the very reverse of promiscuous.'

Tansey nodded. He had hoped that Peter Merger could be crossed off his mental list of those who might have been involved in Hannah's disappearance, but it was clear that this was not possible—at least for the moment. And, only too aware that he was still far from an answer to the problem, Tansey brought the interview with Peter Merger to a close, and sent for Sergeant Abbot.

Abbot had not been idle in the interval. He had spent a while on the telephone, with a certain amount of success. He had also talked to WPC Reid who had been tracing Hannah's movements in Oxford the previous Friday afternoon. And he had coped with an irate Granny Hayne—an experience which had proved very satisfactory from his point of view. But he was careful not to demonstrate his self-satisfaction to Tansey.

He started with the report of the woman police constable. 'WPC Reid has returned to Headquarters, sir. She's compiling her report now. As we expected, she had very little trouble. Briefly, Hannah arrived in Oxford by bus at two-thirty on Friday. She went straight to the Banbury abortion clinic, whose staff incidentally gave WPC Reid every assistance. Hannah had phoned earlier to make an appointment for a preliminary examination. She had said her name was Anne Chanter, so the clinic had made no connection with the missing Hannah Aston. She was given the usual information as to what was required and what to expect, but had suddenly walked out just before she was due to see the doctor. Presumably she had changed her mind; it does happen sometimes, they said.

'When Hannah was next seen,' Abbot went on, 'she was with an older man, having tea at the Willow Café in Ship Street. According to the waitress they appeared to know each other well, and she saw him pat Hannah's hand. The man's description fits Morgan Browne, sir.'

Tansey nodded. 'I'm not surprised. We have further confirmation from Peter Merger that Browne and Hannah were together on Friday. I think we need to have a serious talk with Mr Browne, Abbot. The Housemaster's got some explaining to do.'

'He has indeed, sir. I was wondering . . .' Abbot paused. 'There was a phone call from that young man Stanley Tranter, sir. He says that someone was blundering around in the shrubbery on Saturday night, and that Alan Carson and two other people—by which I assume he meant himself and his girlfriend—saw a 'ghost'. He described it as about six feet tall, and substantial, either a master or a senior boy. The odd thing was that this ghost bolted as soon as it saw them. And what I was wondering, sir, was if it could have been Mr Browne, with a sheet over his costume as a sort of second disguise.'

'Hm-m.' Tansey considered the possibility. 'It's an intriguing idea, Sergeant, but of course it could be applied to persons other than Browne. Anyway, as I said, we need a quiet talk with him, and preferably not in the presence of his wife. Anything else?'

'Yes, sir. Old Granny Hayne turned up.'

'Here? At HQ?'

'Yes, sir. She demanded to see the Chief Constable, but was persuaded to settle for me.' Abbot couldn't prevent himself from grinning. Then he suddenly became serious. 'She's over eighty, you know, sir, and she doesn't get around much. This was a major expedition for her.'

'What did she want?'

'To complain about police brutality, sir. According to her, Sergeant Donaldson arrived at her house—it's a cottage really—yesterday morning with another police officer and proceeded to interrogate Nick. 'Like them Gestapos,' she said. He wanted to search the place, but she wouldn't let them in without a warrant. The old girl knows her rights. Anyway she saw them off the premises, but this morning discovered that Nick had decamped in the middle of the night and she blames us—or rather Sergeant Donaldson.'

'Damn!' said Tansey, and repeated, 'Damn it! Now we'll have the job of finding Nick, and if by some chance there was anything in the cottage connecting Nick and Hannah it'll have vanished into thin air. Is the old girl still here?'

'No, sir. I gave her a cup of tea and sent her home in a police car. I hope that was right?'

'Yes, Abbot.' Tansey sighed. 'I expect you dealt with her a good deal better than I would have done.' He went on to recount what Peter Merger had told him. 'It means Merger has no alibi for Saturday night. I'm sure the Fanshawes will confirm his story, but it doesn't cover him. Mind you, it's difficult to imagine him doing away with Hannah and then going off with his new girlfriend, but killers have done stranger things before now.'

'But what could his motive be, sir? As far as we know he and Hannah ceased to have any kind of relationship—however innocuous—once Hannah went to Coriston, and that's at least a couple of years ago.'

'I suppose they could have been seeing each other secretly,' said Tansey, 'though Peter's apparently got this new girlfriend. In any case, you're right about motive, Sergeant. Even if he had made Hannah pregnant the Astons would probably have been unpleasant, but not even Mrs Aston could have suggested it was rape and accused him of committing a crime.'

The Chief Inspector thought in silence for a few minutes. Then he added, 'It's perfectly possible that it wasn't Hannah's lover who killed her. One far-fetched scenario is that Merger could have found out about him, and about the pregnancy; she might even have told him herself. He could have been consumed by jealousy, as they used to say. No, I'm not accusing Peter Merger, Abbot. I'm keeping an open mind—and still hoping Hannah may be found alive, though I must confess it's a steadily diminishing hope.'

And by the end of the day the hope had become negligible.

As darkness fell, and the search of woods and ditches became impossible, a police officer examining the broken fencing around the old quarry found some strands of grey artificial hair which it was expected would prove to be part of Hannah Aston's Hallowe'en costume.

CHAPTER 14

The next day was a Thursday, an unimportant fact, except that it happened to be the Fifth of November, Guy Fawkes Day. Several years ago this uniquely English celebration of a failed attempt to blow up the Palace of Westminster had ended in tragedy in Colombury. A vagrant rocket had set fire to the thatched roof of a cottage, the fire had spread, two houses and a shop had been burned down and a mother had died trying in vain to rescue her children from their smoke-filled bedroom.

Since then, although it was impossible to prevent the purchase of fireworks in Oxford or elsewhere, by unspoken common consent the celebration had in Colombury become a semi-official public event, and private bonfires and firework displays were frowned upon—so much so in fact that fireworks were not stocked in local shops.

Thus it was that, during the week following Hannah's disappearance, an ever-growing heap of combustible rubbish had been under construction in the middle of a large field on the outskirts of the town. By Thursday it was over ten feet high and on its summit sat a Guy, resplendent in an old pink hunting jacket, yellowing breeches and a top hat.

The crowds began to gather soon after seven o'clock in the evening, and by eight when the show began there were three or four hundred people assembled around three sides of the field. Some of these, such as the Reverend and Mrs Weston, the Mergers, Dr Fenwick and Audrey and Rodney Driver were regular attendants.

Others who usually came were not there this year. Nick Hayne was missing, as were the Astons and of course

Hannah. But there were some new faces. Bill Eversley had brought Marjorie and, in an effort to relieve the gloom that seemed to have settled over Coriston, Dr Sheringham had as a special favour allowed a party of senior pupils to be present, in the charge of Miss Price and Mr Blondel, who had nobly volunteered for this duty.

The police were also represented; in fact, one of the constables with some explosives training was in charge of the fireworks, while Sergeant Donaldson and a few other officers were there in their official capacities to ensure that order was maintained, that adequate safety measures were taken and that there was no illicit drinking by minors or drug-taking by anyone. In addition, Chief Inspector Tansey, told of the event by Donaldson, had decided on the spur of the moment to attend; his wife, Hilary, and their child were visiting her parents and the house was cheerless without them. He was surprised that so many people knew him.

The vicar wished him a good-evening and so did Dr Fenwick. Peter Merger gave him a friendly nod, and Alex Merger introduced his wife, Rose. They chatted for a couple of minutes without mentioning Hannah. The Drivers were not so tactful, though at first they seemed to be absorbed in their own affairs.

'Hello, Chief Inspector,' Rodney Driver hailed Tansey exuberantly. 'Lovely night, isn't it? Look at those stars. We're in luck. It could have been wet and windy.'

'It's none too warm,' said Tansey.

'There's coffee and a hot dog stand over there.' Audrey pointed. Wrapped in a variety of woollen garments, she looked shorter and squarer than ever beside her elegant husband. 'And, of course, a queue,' she added.

'It's best to bring a flask on these occasions,' said Rodney, grinning.

Tansey returned the grin. 'You're very cheerful tonight,' he remarked.

'Our fortunes have changed.' Driver explained that a neighbour who owned horses, hearing of their difficulty, had offered to lend them a substitute for Vain Glory for as long as was necessary. 'Terribly good of him. It's solved all our problems. We needn't have worried,' he said with satisfaction.

'You're lucky,' Tansey wished that his own problems could be so easily solved.

'Except for paying an enormous vet's bill,' Audrey reminded her husband bitterly. 'We've got Hannah to thank for that still.'

The conversation was suddenly interrupted by a salvo of rockets that streaked across the night sky. Then there was a 'whoosh' as a red star rose from a mound at the far side of the field and, reaching its apogee, released a burst of further stars which each exploded into a saffron spray of light. It was followed by another and another until the sky was ablaze and crackling with noise. Everyone applauded the start of the firework display.

The interruption allowed Tansey to ignore Audrey Driver's last remark but, as the Drivers drifted away from him to join friends, he began to question himself. So far in this investigation he had concentrated on the men—Browne, Driver, Peter Merger, for example—He hadn't considered a combination of Audrey and Rodney Driver, or Audrey alone. She might well have had more than one reason for hating Hannah, and there was no cause to suppose she hadn't the ability to destroy her.

And then there was Shirley Browne. When he had talked to Morgan earlier in the day, the Housemaster had explained how he had come to meet Hannah in Oxford on Friday afternoon, but admitted that he hadn't told his wife about the encounter. He had kept quiet, he said, because his marriage was 'not very comfortable at present'. But Mrs Browne could easily have learnt of the meeting and drawn her own conclusions—especially from her husband's silence. Tansey stared unseeing at a large Catherine wheel which spluttered round and round without respite, as if the poor saint were still tied to it.

'Hello, Chief Inspector,' a voice behind him broke in on his musing. 'You got my phone message?'

Tansey turned and in the flickering light of the fireworks recognized Stanley Tranter. 'Yes, thanks.'

'I take it that that's the end of the matter—as far as I'm concerned?'

'I hope so,' Tansey said coldly, disliking the young man, 'but I can't promise. This is a murder inquiry.'

There was a quick catch of breath and Tranter said, 'You've found her?'

'Not yet.'

Thinking that Stanley Tranter was perhaps not as indifferent to Hannah as he sounded, Tansey turned back to watch the display. But he was not left alone with his thoughts for long. This time the interruption came from Marjorie Eversley.

'Chief Inspector, I want you to meet Dad.'

'Bill Eversley.' The man beside her held out his hand. 'Chief Inspector, I owe you an apology. I know you've been trying to get in touch with me, but I really have been extraordinarily busy and I suspected I could add nothing to what my wife and Marjorie have already told you.'

Tansey shook the proffered hand. Apart from the fact that he was of medium height and wearing an expensive sheepskin coat, it was difficult to get much of an impression of the lawyer. But he had a pleasant assured voice, and the apology had sounded genuine.

'This is a bad business,' Eversley continued. 'I suppose there's no more news of Hannah?'

'We're now treating it as a case of murder, Mr Eversley.'

'I was afraid it would come to that.' Eversley was sombre. 'I blame myself. With hindsight I can't imagine why I went off and left the girl. I should have made a fuss, but Marjorie was so sure she must have gone already, and—'

A burst of firecrackers drowned the rest of his words, but it wasn't difficult to guess them. Tansey said, 'Mr Eversley, it's impossible to think or talk in these circumstances. Perhaps you could spare me some time tomorrow?'

'That's just what I was going to suggest. Tomorrow morning? Shall we say nine? In my office? I repeat that I very much doubt if I can offer any new information, but maybe I can confirm some of what you already know.'

'Thanks,' said Tansey. 'I'll be there,' and he thought that at least the evening had not been a complete waste of time since Eversley had finally been pinned down.

With a wave of his hand Bill Eversley went after his daughter who had gone to speak to Rod Driver, and simultaneously there was a last salvo of rockets like an artillery barrage as the firework display came to an end. Then a booming voice sounded over a loud-hailer.

'Ladies and gentlemen, I hope you've all enjoyed our little show. It may not be the greatest salute that Guy Fawkes has received this evening, but I'm sure you'll agree it was a fine effort for Colombury, and we're very grateful to those who've helped to organize it. Let's give them a cheer—and then I'll be lighting this magnificent bonfire and burning our handsome Guy.'

As the cheering exploded into the night Dick Tansey decided that he had had enough, and started to make his way towards the field's exit and the car park. But everyone else seemed to be moving, and with people being urged to stand well back and make a large circle before the bonfire was lit, he made little headway. Abandoning the idea for the moment, he found himself standing near Stephen Blondel and some Coriston seniors.

'Chief Inspector, is there any news?' Blondel asked at once, and before Tansey could answer added, 'It seems dreadful that we should be here enjoying ourselves when Hannah—someone we saw nearly every day and worked with and liked—is probably lying dead somewhere. I didn't agree with Dr Sheringham's decision, but—'

He stopped as the bonfire, liberally doused with paraffin, caught alight and started to burn merrily. There was some rhythmic clapping and as the flames reached the Guy a great cheer. Then as the stuffed figure shifted on its pyre something fell out of the blazing mound on to the grass.

And there was a wild, desperate cry, 'Hannah! Hannah's shoe!'

Tansey recognized Marjorie Eversley's voice, but he was slow to act. Before he had moved Stephen Blondel and Rodney Driver had forestalled him. Of the two, Blondel was the swifter, but he was also inept. Reaching the smouldering object, he stumbled and kicked it hard into the bottom of the conflagration, where Driver prodded at it ineffectively with the walking stick he was carrying.

By now they were joined by Tansey and one of the organizers, whose task seemed to be to rake any loose bits that fell from the bonfire off the surrounding grass, so as to keep the pyre tidy, and prevent the fire from spreading.

'Back! Back!' The official was waving his rake.

'Get that object out of there!' Tansey gave his authoritative counter order.

Tansey had been expecting to meet with minor officiousness, but to his surprise the man not only grasped what was wanted of him, but obeyed immediately, and in a few moments what had once been a part of Hannah Aston's Hallowe'en gear lay smouldering on the ground. It was still recognizable as a shoe, and attached to it was a large, square buckle set with coloured stones, which had suffered less from the fire than might have been expected.

'Who's meant to be in charge here?' Tansey demanded.

'I am,' said the efficient individual with the rake. 'I'm Councillor Grosmith.'

'Good. I'm Detective Chief Inspector Tansey, and this object is police evidence. Can you get me a bucket of water or something similar in which I can stop it burning, and could you fetch Sergeant Donaldson? He's around somewhere.'

'I know where there's a bucket,' Driver volunteered.

Once more Grosmith asked no questions. 'Right,' he said. 'You get it, and I'll find Donaldson.'

'Chief Inspector, I am so sorry,' said Blondel as they were left together. 'That was careless of me. The light of the flames caught my spectacles for a second and I couldn't see. Thank goodness it wasn't destroyed.'

'No damage done, Mr Blondel—luckily,' said Tansey, who thought that this was no thanks to Blondel or to Driver; they had both proved to be singularly inefficient. Or had one of them acted purposefully, determined that the shoe should be destroyed?

He looked at the bonfire, still watched by the crowd, few of whom seemed to have appreciated the significance of the incident that had just taken place. It was now burning fiercely, and he wondered what other evidence it might be consuming. But nothing could be done about that, at least for the present.

Certain preliminary actions could, however, be taken and, when Rodney Driver arrived with a bucket, closely followed by Sergeant Donaldson and Mr Grosmith, the Chief Inspector issued the necessary instructions. First the shoe, or what remained of it, was carefully lifted into the bucket with the rake, and Tansey took charge of this evidence. He hesitated for a moment and then, thinking that soaking ashes would present forensic with a difficult task, ordered that the bonfire must not be doused, but allowed to die down of its own accord. However, once it was out the ashes were to be covered with a waterproof tarpaulin to protect any further evidence. The site should be left untouched till morning, when the ashes would be examined minutely and collected for forensic examination. Two police officers would be required to guard the area during the night. Sergeant Donaldson would be responsible.

They had all listened to Tansey in silence, but when he had finished speaking Rodney Driver asked the obvious question. 'You—you don't think Hannah is—was—in there, do you?'

'No!' The exclamation seemed forced from Stephen Blondel. 'What a ghastly thought! Ghastly!'

'And not possible.' Mr Grosmith was reassuring. 'I supervised the building of that bonfire myself. We started on Tuesday, and it was done in stages. It's quite a skilled job. No one could have come along and pushed a body in there without my noticing it. Small objects, yes—but not a body.'

'Thank God for that,' said Blondel.

There was a murmur of agreement. And Tansey thought how useful and cooperative the Councillor had been; the times in which the shoe—or anything else—could have been thrust into the bonfire had been narrowed to Tuesday and Wednesday, presumably after dark. He nodded to Sergeant Donaldson to get on with his job, dismissed as a waste of breath the notion of asking Blondel and Driver not to mention the shoe to anyone, and asked Mr Grosmith to be good enough to stand by until Donaldson's return in case anything else fell out of the fire. Then he took the bucket over to the Eversleys.

Marjorie was standing with her face pressed into her

father's chest, and his arms were around her. 'I wish to God we'd never come,' Bill Eversley said.

'I'm glad you did,' said Tansey. 'It was quick of Marjorie to spot that was one of Hannah's shoes. Probably the other one's in the bonfire too. But listen, Marjorie, they're only shoes. Not Hannah. Hannah's not there. I doubt if she's ever been anywhere near here.'

Marjorie lifted her head. 'Are you sure?'

'Positive!' said Tansey, thankful that it wasn't a lie. 'But, Marjorie, I must ask you to do something. Please look at this and tell me if you can identify it for certain as one of Hannah's witch's shoes.' He produced a small torch from his pocket and shone it into the bucket.

'All right.' Marjorie gave the burnt remains of the shoe a long look. 'Yes, Chief Inspector. I'm certain. There can't be another pair like that. I was with Hannah when she bought them. It was at the Oxfam shop in Colombury. They were in the window and she said, "They'll be just right for a witch with those pointed toes and that gaudy buckle." So we went in and bought them. I remember she didn't have enough money and I lent her some.' Majorie's voice broke and she started to cry. 'Poor Hannah! She was the dearest friend I've ever had.'

'She had a good friend in you, too, Marjorie,' Tansey said. 'When we find the person who harmed her, it'll be partly thanks to you.'

Marjorie gave him a watery smile and Eversley said, 'Come along, girl, time for home and bed. Ma will be getting worried about us.' Nodding goodnight to Tansey, he added, 'See you in the morning, Chief Inspector.'

'Yes. Good night to you both,' Tansey replied.

By now the bonfire was dying down and many people were leaving, especially those with smaller children. Stephen Blondel and Beth Price were collecting the Coriston contingent. Chief Inspector Tansey checked that

Sergeant Donaldson was carrying out his instructions, expressed hearty thanks to Councillor Grosmith for his understanding and cooperation as he said good night, and took the bucket off to his car.

It had been, he thought, an unexpectedly interesting—even illuminating—evening, and tomorrow promised further developments. He reflected on the unintended pun, as he realized that he no longer doubted that Hannah was dead. She had been killed, and afterwards her killer, finding he still had her incriminating shoe in his possession, had tried to get rid of it in the bonfire. At least this suggested that the villain was someone with local knowledge and no passing stranger.

CHAPTER 15

At noon the following day one of the police divers at the disused quarry near Shipton surfaced and signalled that he had found a body. The officers standing by swung into action. It had been impossible to conceal the fact that the police intended to send divers into the quarry, and the media were present in force. Inevitably too there were some sightseers—the merely curious and others who had known and been fond of Hannah. Everyone had been kept at a distance from the scene of operations, but now they were pushed back further, the whole area of the quarry cordoned off and screens erected. This did not prevent the whirring of cameras and a general gasp of sympathy as the meaning of this activity became apparent.

Chief Inspector Tansey had arrived at the scene with Sergeant Abbot half an hour earlier. They had spent a busy morning. First they had gone to Bill Eversley's office, where he had answered all their questions freely, but added nothing to what they already knew. They had been about to leave when Tansey had suddenly turned and asked if the Eversley family, apart from Marjorie, had liked Hannah, and what they had really thought of her.

Eversley appeared to give the question serious reflection. 'My sons didn't like her,' he said at last. 'I gather they considered her a prude. There was an unfortunate incident once when they were teasing her. Harold, my younger boy, tried to give her a French kiss, and she smacked him quite violently across the face. But Mary and I were sorry for her. The Astons are a strict couple, rather old-fashioned, and without too much money, but with great ambitions for Hannah. Personally I don't believe she was a happy child, though she had a lot going for her, and certainly Marjorie was extremely fond of her.'

'That's very clear, Mr Eversley,' said the Chief Inspector. 'Thank you.'

Bill Eversley had had one further comment. 'Chief Inspector, if this has been a local crime—and that shoe in the bonfire suggests it was—the sooner it's cleared up the better, as I'm sure you'll agree.'

Recalling what Bill Eversley had said, Tansey agreed wholeheartedly as he looked down at the dead Hannah's black-stockinged feet. She had risen to the surface of her own accord, once her hair had been disentangled from the rusty remains of a bicycle. In addition to her black stockings, she was still wearing her witch's costume, including her black pointed hat, tied on securely by means of its false hair. Her shoes, however, were missing, She was a dreadful sight, bloated and ugly.

Yes, thought Tansey, the sooner the better, for everyone's sake, but he couldn't accomplish the impossible. It was less than a week since he had first heard of Hannah Aston, and at least some answers had been found.

He sighed, and turned to an officer beside him. 'OK,' he

said at last. 'Get on to Kidlington. All the usual. Dr Band, the pathologist, a scene of crime team, photographers, the forensic boys, lighting and a generator just in case. Oh, and we'd better have an incident van, again just in case we're here some time.'

It was not long before the area was a hive of activity. Dr Band arrived, having been brought from his surgery. All he could do was pronounce the obvious—that the girl was dead—and point out to Tansey the fading bruises on her neck. The rest was for the pathologist, who was on his way to view the body before it was moved from the spot where it had been dragged from the water. It was ridiculous, Tansey knew—the man could do nothing until the body had reached the mortuary—but procedures were procedures.

Tansey had one further thought. He approached the officer in charge of the divers. 'Could they go down again, and search for a shoe—just one—black and with a large buckle?'

The Chief Inspector was apologetic. It might be their job, but it was a lousy job, and they had been working since first light that morning. Nevertheless, it had to be done. No sign of the other shoe—or for that matter of anything else remotely connected with Hannah—had emerged from a meticulous examination of the bonfire's remains on the site, and it was most unlikely that the forensic examination of the ashes would disclose anything useful.

So the divers dived yet again, and Tansey watched and waited. The day that had started fine had clouded over, and drops of rain were now beginning to fall. The pathologist—one Dr Ghent—arrived from Oxford, inspected and examined the body briefly, conferred with Tansey and Dr Band and departed, followed by the ambulance containing all that remained of Hannah.

Tansey, on being told that the spectators were leaving, went outside the cordon to speak to the press. All he could say was that, as must have been obvious, a body had been found in the quarry; he had nothing to add until identification had been confirmed and the next-of-kin informed, or until the formal report on the cause of death had been received. He was brusque as he brushed aside the shouted questions.

He looked around during his short briefing and noticed Peter Merger among the group of dispersing spectators. Then, glancing across the quarry to where the ground rose in a gentle slope towards the rolling hills, he saw a horse and rider silhouetted against the sky. The man was too far away to be recognized, but Tansey suspected that he was Rodney Driver, and he remembered the old saying that murderers often returned to the scene of the crime. It was not an adage in which he had much faith.

Fifteen minutes later the divers were about to abandon their search when one of them, moving a bit of junk, discovered the missing shoe. There was no buckle attached to it, and a further concerted effort did not produce one.

'It *could* be down there, sir,' said the senior diver, who had found the shoe, 'but there's so much rubbish—old mattresses, fridges, bits of cars, you name it—we could take a month of Sundays and still miss a little buckle.'

'I know,' Tansey said. 'You've all done splendidly, and I'm very grateful.'

The scene of crime officer appeared beside him. 'What now?' he asked. 'A fingertip search?'

'I can't see any alternative,' replied Tansey, 'at least in the immediate area—say a hundred yards around the quarry, and especially towards the road. Car tracks, signs of a body being dragged or carried, this damned buckle—anything. You know as well as I do what we're after. I'll leave you to it. Good luck.'

'What are the odds that buckle will ever turn up, sir?' Abbot asked as they drove away from the quarry.

'I wouldn't bet on it.' Tansey was thoughtful. 'And don't forget that Nick Hayne hasn't turned up yet either. Abbot, I'm going to drop you off in Colombury, I want you to go and have a chat with Granny Hayne, see if you can get anything more out of her. Make it a friendly call.'

'I'll do my best, sir,' Abbot said doubtfully. 'Nick's a funny guy but I don't believe he's involved in this affair. Hannah wouldn't have gone with him of her own accord since she was scared of him, and I can't imagine him abducting her from Coriston.'

'Maybe not, but we need to have a talk with him.'

'Yes, sir, of course. What shall I do after Granny Hayne?'

'Meet me at the Windrush Arms, and be thankful, Sergeant. You may not relish the old girl, but you're luckier than I am. I'll tell you what I'm proposing to do—collect WPC Lasington, who isn't too young and is a kindly woman, and take her with me when I break the news to the Astons. You and I both know there's no doubt about identification, and it's not fair to keep them in suspense any longer than necessary. I'll leave Lasington with them while they get over the shock. Even though they must fear that Hannah's dead, it will still come as a blow. Lasington can help them cope with practicalities like getting friends and family. Then this afternoon I hope we can take Major Aston into Oxford to identify the body formally.'

'Yes, sir.' Abbot grinned sympathetically. 'I'll settle for Granny Hayne any day, and I'll be waiting for you at the Windrush Arms, ready with a couple of pints.'

'Which I'll certainly need,' said Tansey, thankful to have an understanding sergeant.

'How did the Astons take it, sir?' Abbot asked later, when they had met again.

Tansey shrugged. 'Much as you'd expect. The Astons

are the sort of people who believe in keeping a stiff upper lip, at least in public.'

The two police officers were sitting at a corner table in the bar of the Windrush Arms, a plate of sandwiches and pints of beer in front of them. The bar was fairly full, but the conversation was subdued. Clearly the news had spread, and it was easy to guess the subject that was uppermost in most of the drinkers' minds. Occasionally one or other of them cast a curious glance in the direction of Tansey and Abbot, but no one intruded on them.

'We're picking the Major up at two-thirty and taking him to the mortuary,' Tansey said, opening a sandwich and inspecting with approval the generous amount of ham it contained.

Abbot nodded, his own mouth full. 'Right.'

'Now, how did you get on with Granny Hayne?'

'She was quite affable, but not forthcoming.' Abbot frowned. 'She was busy sewing.'

'Sewing?'

'Yes, sir. She's got an ancient machine that's practically a museum piece. When I asked her what she was making, she said she was mending a sheet, putting sides to middle, which is what I remember my own gran doing years ago, but nowadays . . . Anyway, sir, I said nothing, but it made me think.'

'It makes me think, too,' said Tansey, and thought of a 'ghost' over six feet high, a 'ghost' that could be frightened by Monica Vaughan and Stanley Tranter. All that a big hulking Nick would have needed was a sheet with holes cut in the middle. But what was he doing—if it *was* Nick Hayne—at Coriston College's Hallowe'en party? And what might he have seen?

'Abbot, the old girl didn't give you any clue where Nick might be?'

'No, sir, and I got the impression, though I could be

wrong, that she had no idea and was really worried.'

Absent-mindedly Tansey pushed the last sandwich towards Abbot, and drained his beer. How imperative was it that Nick should be found? There was nothing against the young man, except for Hannah's seemingly unreasonable fear of him, the fact that he had disappeared, perhaps scared of the police, and now the business of the sheet, which could be quite irrelevant.

Given unlimited manpower the Chief Inspector wouldn't have hesitated, but there was no point in wishful thinking. A practical decision had to be made, and Tansey was well aware that not only might his future promotion depend on such a decision—and he was human enough to consider this factor—but a killer might remain free to strike again.

'Sir, if we're to pick up the Major at two-thirty, we should perhaps consider going,' Abbot said, breaking in on Tansey's ruminations.

'Yes,' Tansey agreed, 'Let's go. The beer and the sandwiches were fine, but our presence here doesn't seem to have added to the gaiety of the place.'

They were on the pavement outside the Windrush Arms when the Reverend William Weston, eyes on the ground and thoughts elsewhere, literally bumped into them. Realizing whom he had come upon, Weston seized Tansey by the arm and almost shook him.

'God moves in a mysterious way,' he said. 'Chief Inspector, ever since Hannah Aston disappeared I've been in a moral dilemma. I've thought about it, and I've prayed. Now, meeting you suddenly like this seems to have resolved my problem.'

'It has?' Tansey had no idea what Weston was talking about, but experience had taught him that people were often troubled about giving information to the police, either because they believed it would be misinterpreted or disregarded, or because they feared it was pointing a finger at someone who might be innocent. 'Good. Do you want to discuss it with me?'

'Yes, yes, of course. That's what I mean. But alone, Chief Inspector.' Weston shot a dubious glance at Sergeant Abbot. 'It's for your ears only. Come along to the vicarage with me. We can't talk in the street.'

Tansey hesitated. He didn't want to be late picking up Major Aston, but the vicar might change his mind. 'All right,' he said, and to Abbot, 'You go and fetch the Major, Sergeant. Meet me outside the church.'

'Yes, sir.'

'Poor Richard has to identify the body, he told me,' Weston said as he and Tansey walked along to St Michael's. 'A dreadful tragedy this, Chief Inspector, a dreadful tragedy, and there's so little we can do to help. We hurried to the Astons as soon as we heard that Hannah had been found, and my wife's there now as well as that nice policewoman. Richard's sent for Irene's sister, and she'll arrive tomorrow, which Irene should find some consolation, but . . . ' He shook his head sadly.

At the vicarage next to the church Weston led the way to his study. Motioning Tansey to a chair, he himself remained standing. He seemed to have difficulty in commencing his tale.

'Mr Weston, I don't want to sound impatient,' Tansey said at last, 'but as you know I've got to take Major Aston in to Oxford this afternoon, so if you'd tell me quite simply what's troubling you I'd be grateful.'

'It's Nick Hayne, Chief Inspector,' Weston said, and once he had begun the words poured from him. 'God knows I don't want to accuse Nick, but there are some facts you should be aware of, and I don't believe you are. Nick killed a girl once. Oh, it was a long time ago. He was only fourteen, and he was provoked and, of course, he's mentally retarded. In the end, I understand there was some kind of hearing and the authorities decided against a proper prosecution, on condition that Nick was sent to an institution—"detained at Her Majesty's pleasure" was the phrase they used, I think. Nick was in this mental home for several years, and I suppose by then he seemed all right. Anyway, they said he could come to live with his grandmother, and until that fight the other day he's always been very peaceful and friendly, but—'

Tansey was staring at the vicar. 'When and where was this, Mr Weston?' he demanded.

'Seven or eight years ago. In Richmond in Yorkshire. I'm not sure about the details. We just happened to learn of it because my wife's brother was at one time a doctor at the mental institution where Nick was sent, and last year when he came to Colombury to stay with us he recognized Nick. No one else in Colombury knows—except Granny Hayne, I suppose—about the girl, I mean. They may know that Nick spent some time in a home, but that's all.'

Tansey was astounded. Naturally, routine checks were being run on the backgrounds of all those connected with the case, but no hint of such a story had surfaced. Maybe it was early days, in spite of computers, he reflected. Maybe, if there was no prosecution . . . Anyway, if his meeting with Weston, God-willed or otherwise, had resolved Weston's problem, it had also resolved his own. A countrywide call must go out at once for Nick Hayne. It should have been done earlier. If only he had known . . .

He said, 'I see. Well, thank you for telling me, Mr Weston. It could be important. May I use your telephone?'

'Of course.' Weston pointed to the phone on the desk. 'I'll leave you to talk in private.'

'Thanks. I shan't be long.'

Indeed, it didn't take the Chief Inspector long to get through to Headquarters and issue orders. Nick Hayne—

detailed description obtainable from Colombury station—was to be found urgently and held for questioning. Details of the killing of the girl in Richmond must be requested from the Yorkshire force. And while all this was set in motion, Tansey thought, his own task was to deal with Major Aston.

The only way was to treat the situation coldly and professionally, Tansey knew. If you showed too much sympathy before the relatives had identified the body they would almost inevitably break down, and this applied to men as much as to women. The answer was to wait quietly until the ordeal was over, and then offer whatever consolation was possible.

But it wasn't always easy to judge in advance what the reaction would be. Tansey glanced anxiously at Major Aston. He had made it his business to get to know the Major's record; his army career had not been exceptional, but Aston had done a couple of tours of duty in Northern Ireland and had presumably seen a dead body before. Nevertheless, he was now ashen-faced, his lower lip trembling, standing unnaturally straight as if at attention and with his fists clenched. He kept his eyes firmly fixed on a distant spot on the mortuary wall.

'Please, Major Aston. You must look at her!'

Slowly Richard Aston lowered his gaze. Hannah lay in what was in fact a large metal drawer. The sheet which had covered her was folded back to reveal her face framed by her once beautiful hair. She had been washed and tidied and was not an unpleasant sight, but rather a kind of caricature of her former self. In death she did not look at peace.

'Hannah? Yes, that's my Hannah.' Richard Aston choked. 'My little girl. My darling one. My own true—'

'Catch him!' Tansey said sharply.

As if in slow motion, Aston's legs were folding. His vision

had grown dark. He was not conscious of falling, but only of the hardness of the floor. Then he was being lifted, carried, and there was blessed nothingness.

When he regained consciousness he was lying on a couch in what was clearly an office. Chief Inspector Tansey was there, and a man in a white coat, the pathologist to whom he had been introduced earlier but whose name he couldn't remember. Very carefully he made an effort to sit up.

The doctor pushed him back. 'A cup of tea, Major Aston?' he said.

'Thank you.' The cup rattled in the saucer as Aston tried to drink it. The tea was hot and sweet, which normally he would have disliked, but in the present circumstances he was thankful for it. He didn't speak until he had finished and Tansey had taken the cup from him. Then he said, 'Hannah didn't—didn't take her own life, did she?'

'No, Major. We'll know more after the post mortem, but I can tell you now that there's every indication that she didn't kill herself, and in all probability she was dead before she was put in the water.'

Aston nodded heavily. 'She was so unhappy, so unhappy,' he muttered. 'She said that if she couldn't have an abortion she'd die rather than have the baby.'

CHAPTER 16

By Saturday morning almost the whole of the population of Colombury was aware that Hannah had been found, and in what circumstances. Reactions among those who had known the girl were varied. There was a general feeling of distress and sympathy for her parents, but few people were deeply touched. And the old cliché that 'life has to go on' was once again proved true.

At Coriston College Dr Sheringham, who previously could scarcely have put a face to Hannah Aston's name, wrote a letter of condolence to Major and Mrs Aston, and had it delivered by hand. Although the following Sunday was Remembrance Sunday and therefore hardly a suitable occasion for the expression of personal grief, he also arranged that at the chapel morning service a mention should be made of Hannah's death and a prayer said for the Astons.

Otherwise it was a normal term-time Saturday at Coriston. Most of the students who didn't have exeats were playing games or cheering on their Houses. A few were studying. Stanley Tranter was working on the novel he was secretly writing. Morgan Browne, who had at last rather reluctantly told Shirley of his meeting with Hannah in Oxford and had found her reaction surprisingly understanding, was giving his scholarship boys some extra coaching. Stephen Blondel was cleaning his car.

At the Drivers' riding school it was also business as usual. All the horses, with the exception of Vain Glory, now convalescing, were out. Mrs Eversley had phoned to say that Marjorie was too upset at Hannah's death to take her lesson, and Audrey had replied that in the circumstances she had not expected Marjorie to come.

But Alan Carson was there, feeling aggrieved; he had been snubbed by both the Drivers.

'Sad about Hannah, isn't it?' he had said on his arrival in the stable yard. 'I suppose you've heard the rumour that she was pregnant?'

'Very sad,' Rodney said shortly, his face unsmiling.

'And, if you've any common sense, Alan,' Audrey added, 'you won't repeat that rumour.'

'Yes. Maybe you're right. Anyway, it's probably untrue.' Alan shrugged. 'Hannah didn't much appreciate being touched up. Not even by Rod,' he added so softly that

Audrey was not sure if she had heard him correctly.

And while the Drivers and all the others went about their business, the Astons, who were naturally the most affected by Hannah's death, were also doing their best to behave normally, at least superficially. It was far from easy. Their telephone calls were intercepted and the police presence outside the house had been doubled in order to keep away the media representatives and the merely curious. But there were some phone calls that had to be taken, two or three letters were hand-delivered, and flowers arrived from a couple of sympathizers. Undoubtedly, there would be more to come. Irene and Richard, who wanted only to be left alone, got the impression that they were under siege.

At two o'clock Irene suddenly said that she was going to meet her sister's train, though Priscilla had said that she would take a taxi from the station. Richard made only the briefest objection. He knew that Irene would do exactly what she wanted, and in fact he was glad to have time to himself. He was half way through a letter he was writing, and now he could complete it in peace, ready for posting the next day.

When the two women arrived he went into the hall to greet them, wearing an apron and rubber gloves. Priscilla, who was fair and blue-eyed like Irene, but looked younger though in fact she was three years older, burst out laughing at his appearance.

'What on earth are you doing, Richard?' she said as she kissed him on the cheek, noticing with approval that he had shaved well. She had already privately appraised Irene and now reached the conclusion that they were both 'making an effort'. She grieved for them, of course. She was sorry about Hannah—it was a dreadful thing to have happened—but Hannah had never been her favourite niece, and to her it was not a really personal tragedy. She was there to help Irene—and Richard—through this trying period.

After that, they would have to reconsider the situation.

'Sorry, Pris, but you caught me cleaning my medals. It's Remembrance Sunday tomorrow, and we—the British Legion—have the usual parade to the war memorial and a service in St Michael's afterwards. It's amazing how many from Colombury and the villages around have fought and died for their country.'

'And you're going, Richard?' There was approval in Priscilla's voice. She might have married a businessman, but she had been brought up in an army family. 'You always go?'

'Ever since we've been here,' Richard said.

As far as Detective Chief Inspector Tansey was concerned, that Saturday was officially a so-called rest day. He was off duty, though on call as always, and Inspector Whitelaw was the senior officer in charge of the Aston case. In fact, Tansey was seated at his desk in his office at Headquarters. Hilary was not due to return until Wednesday, the house was already moderately tidy for her, and Dick Tansey was restless.

It was barely a week since Hannah had gone missing and less than twenty-four hours since her body had been found. A lot had been accomplished in that period. Indeed, far more progress had been made than was usual in such a short time. Nevertheless, Tansey was dissatisfied, which was the reason why his desk and the floor nearby were piled with files.

He couldn't help feeling that he had missed something vital. It was not what anyone could call a clue, but rather a failure to understand—to appreciate—some of the nuances of what he was being told. Hannah, of course, was at the core of the matter. She hadn't been a casual victim. She had almost certainly been killed because of what she was and how she related to the killer—male or female or even plural, for Tansey had not ruled out any possibilities. But this relationship surely depended largely on the kind of girl Hannah had been.

And what had Hannah Aston been? Tansey had not so far been able to find a simple answer to this vital question; he had no picture in his mind of anything beyond Hannah Aston's physical appearance. All deeper signs seemed contradictory. And this was why on this Saturday morning, when he could have been lying in bed or sweeping up the leaves in his garden, Tansey was poring over the files, a cup of coffee growing cold beside him.

Hannah, when she died, had been almost seventeen. She hadn't been pretty in the usually accepted sense, but she had been striking. Her long corn-coloured hair and her violet eyes had attracted attention. And she had been a clever girl, expecting to go to university. Meanwhile she had a comfortable, if not a rich girl's, home and apparently fond if over-ambitious parents; she had the advantages of a good school and she enjoyed pastimes like acting and riding. She had had 'a lot going for her,' as Bill Eversley had remarked, and her future had been full of promise.

Why, then, had she been unhappy, even before she became pregnant. Had she, as the only child of strict and possibly dull parents, been lonely? In spite of what Irene Aston had said about her having plenty of friends of both sexes, only Peter Merger and Marjorie Eversley had spoken of her with any affection. There had been the odd little story of her reaction to the teasing of Marjorie's brothers, and Stephen Tranter had described her as a '*noli me tangere*' type. Even Peter Merger had sworn that he and Hannah had never made love together, and indeed that Hannah had not been inclined to be responsive—though that could be because at the time she had known herself to be below the age of consent.

Tansey sighed. Clearly Hannah had not been a promiscuous girl—rather the reverse. But somehow she had managed to get herself pregnant. Either she had voluntarily entered into a relationship, or she had been raped. Unbidden, the thought of Nick Hayne came into Tansey's mind. Hannah was the sort of girl who might consider that being raped constituted a personal disgrace, and the possibility of bearing a mentally deficient child would have been abhorrent to her. Feelings of this kind would certainly explain why she had reportedly said to her father that, if an abortion couldn't be arranged without her mother knowing, she would rather die than have the baby.

But there had been nothing in the police records to suggest that Nick Hayne had attempted to rape the girl whom he had killed when he was a minor. Tansey had been lucky enough to speak to a police officer in Richmond who remembered the case. Quite apart from Hayne's age and admitted mental instability, the death had been almost accidental—unlawful killing, perhaps even manslaughter—certainly not murder. The girl had teased him, provoked him and had unfortunately hit her head on a stone ledge when he finally attacked her. There had never been any question of a prosecution, even in a juvenile court.

Suddenly the door of Tansey's office burst open, 'Oh Lord, sorry! I didn't know you were here.' Inspector Whitelaw regarded the heaped files with dismay.

'Come in, Colin. I'm not here officially.'

'I was going to put a note on your desk.' Whitelaw grinned. 'There wouldn't seem to be much room.'

'If it was a mere note it can't be wildly important. Sit down and tell me.'

'I've been to Shipton. I thought I'd check up myself on Julie Fanshawe, Peter Merger's current girlfriend.'

'She corroborated his story?'

'Yes, but there's more to it than that. I had a pint in the local, and the publican was talkative. I'd guess he knows most of what goes on in the village. Julie Fanshawe and

Peter have been going together—walking out, I think it used to be called—for over a year, and it's agreed by all concerned that the relationship is serious, and they'll soon be putting up the banns—if they still bother to do that. But what I'm getting at is this. It would seem extremely unlikely that Peter Merger would have had the time or the opportunity—or for that matter the inclination—to carry on his romance with Hannah in secret, at least during the last twelve months.'

'But she did keep his photo,' Tansey reminded the Inspector.

'Perhaps she forgot she had it.' Whitelaw was not a sentimental man. 'Anyway, she must have found a replacement, mustn't she?'

'Presumably. Any news of Nick Hayne?'

Whitelaw shook his head. ''Fraid not. If Granny Hayne knows where he might be she's not giving. You'd have to pull her fingernails out first. But we've traced the sheet.'

'The sheet?'

'Yes. That sheet Granny Hayne was supposedly putting sides to middle. A lady complained on Monday last that she'd left her washing out on the line last Saturday night—Hallowe'en—and on Sunday morning a sheet was missing. She claims she can identify her sheet by a small stain, and the sheet Granny Hayne was working on has just such a stain.'

'Well, that's great,' said Tansey. 'At least we appear to have identified the ghost in the shrubbery at Coriston. Let's hope it'll help us to identify Hannah's killer.'

Sunday morning. Except for the crucial facts that Hannah's door was shut, that Hannah was not in her room and that Hannah was not coming down to breakfast, it was an ordinary Sunday at the Astons' house. Richard got up at his usual time, took Irene and Priscilla early morning tea and, while he drank his own, re-read the letter he had written the previous day. Satisfied with it, he stuck down the already stamped and addressed envelope, and went upstairs to the bathroom. He would post it at the main office on his way to the parade.

They breakfasted in the kitchen, the Astons both grateful for Priscilla's presence. She was undemanding and, seemingly without effort, she filled in what would have been long gaps in their conversation. Purposely Richard had left the Sunday papers on the hall table; none of them wanted to read about Hannah.

For her part Priscilla thought that Richard was looking better than Irene. He had about him an air of purpose, as if he were prepared to bear his grief with stoicism. On the other hand, Irene, who had admitted on the drive from the station that she had hoped against hope that Hannah was alive until the last possible moment, appeared to have given way to despair and despondency. She had not even protested when Priscilla had said it would be foolish of her to go to church, Remembrance Sunday or not.

'All right,' she agreed. 'You don't mind if I don't come, do you, Richard?'

'No, of course not. We couldn't sit together anyway. I suggest you and Pris watch the Cenotaph ceremony on the telly. Much more satisfactory.'

'Yes.' Irene was apathetic.

Richard left the two women together and went upstairs to change into a dark suit, suitable for the parade. When he returned, wearing his regimental tie, with his medals pinned to his breast pocket, and clutching a neatly-rolled umbrella, he said, 'I'll be off then. Thank goodness it's a fine day. Last year it poured with rain. I should be home about one if Weston doesn't preach for too long.'

Irene shook her head as Richard went to get the car. 'I

don't know how he can be so cheerful, Pris. It's not as if he hadn't been devoted to Hannah. To be honest, she got on better with her father than she did with me.'

'Oh, the relationship between mother and daughter is often uneasy.' Priscilla sought to be supportive. 'But I agree about Richard being more cheerful. He's making a big effort—and it's partly for your sake, Irene.'

Priscilla didn't know how true were her words. It *was* for Irene's sake that Richard was making such an effort. He wouldn't have gone to the parade and the service otherwise.

He arrived at the British Legion Headquarters late. He had sat in the car outside the post office for some minutes before getting out to post his letter, and by the time he arrived at the Legion everyone was busily concerned with last-minute preparations. This was most convenient. People merely nodded and smiled at him, though most kept at a distance. A few who knew him best made their expressions of sympathy brief and understanding. There had just been time to exchange with David Carson the old joke about his failure to buy or borrow the bowler hat which was supposedly *de rigueur* for a former army officer on parade in mufti.

The march through the town and the short service at the war memorial hadn't taxed Richard either. He knew none of the locals who had died in various wars. For him the ceremony was impersonal. But the service at St Michael's which followed was a different matter. On so many Sundays and feast days he had sat in one of the pews towards the front of the church with Hannah beside him that he could imagine her with him now, see her beautiful hair, hear her clear soprano. He buried his face in his hands. His eyes were wet. He tried to pray, but the only words he could find were 'God forgive me'; he repeated these over and over again without meaning.

However, by the time the service was over he had gained control of himself, and he accepted with alacrity Brigadier

Carson's invitation to join him at the Windrush Arms for a snifter. The result was that he smelt strongly of gin by the time he reached home. Nevertheless he insisted that the three of them should have a drink together, and during lunch he told Irene and Priscilla of his morning, trying to make it sound entertaining so that the meal passed pleasantly.

After they had finished coffee, Irene went to their bedroom to rest, while Priscilla filled the dishwasher and then, comfortable in an armchair in the sitting-room, listened to a concert on the radio with the volume low, and started to make a list of all the things that would need to be done during the following week. Richard, having changed into some old clothes, went out into the garden.

Neither of the women heard the noise, but the young police officer on duty at the front door did, and identified it at once as a shot. He also guessed its source, and dashed rapidly into the back garden. A light was on in the garden shed, and it was there that he found Richard Aston slumped over a workbench, a revolver gripped in his right hand. The sight was sickening and he turned away immediately, reaching for his radio.

CHAPTER 17

'Tr-r tr-r! Tr-r tr-r!'

Dick Tansey woke with a start. He had had a large Sunday midday meal with friends and, coming home, had fallen asleep in an armchair, the book he had been reading slipped from his lap to the floor. Now he took a moment to realize where he was. The room was deep in shadows, the curtains still undrawn.

But to respond to the telephone was second nature to

him. He had snapped out his number before he realized that he had risen from his chair to answer the insistent call. He listened intently. It was Inspector Whitelaw calling from Headquarters.

It seemed that Sergeant Donaldson had just been on the blower from Colombury to report that Major Richard Aston had shot himself. A young but competent police officer on duty at the front gate had heard the shot, and had been on the scene of the incident—a garden shed cum workshop at the back of the house—within seconds. The officer had been sensible and had at once informed Sergeant Donaldson, who had in his turn contacted Headquarters.

According to Donaldson, there appeared to be no question of foul play. There was no visible note. It must have been either accident or suicide. Aston had apparently been cleaning a revolver. Nothing had been touched. All Donaldson had done was to send for Dr Band, the police surgeon, to pronounce life extinct, and to organize a police guard. Whitelaw himself was leaving immediately to take charge. He assumed that the Chief Inspector—

'I'm on my way,' said Tansey at once.

'Do you want transport? I could pick you up.'

Tansey thought quickly. It would be inconvenient for Whitelaw and would delay him. He could phone Abbot, but not on a Sunday afternoon, unless it were essential.

'No. I'll drive myself,' he said. 'It'll save time. You get Dr Ghent, the pathologist, and a scene of crime team out there, Inspector. I want to go through the whole routine. Make sure that no one but Band touches the body or anything else till I get there.'

'Sir.'

'Right. An hour or less.'

Tansey's first moves were to put on the kettle and hurry to the bathroom. He felt frowsy and tired after his sleep and needed to wake himself up. He washed his face in cold water and rapidly changed out of his casual clothes. The Chief Constable liked his officers to look smart. By then the kettle had boiled and he made himself a mug of strong tea. While he drank it he considered what Whitelaw had told him.

Accident or suicide? No obvious note. But not all suicides left notes. There could be one in the Major's pocket or under his body; one could even have fallen to the floor. They wouldn't be sure until a thorough search of the garden shed and the house, including especially the Major's study, had been conducted. It was too early yet to surmise.

When Tansey arrived at the Astons' house the lane leading to it was already blocked with cars and police vans, and he drew over on to the verge behind the last vehicle and walked to the front gate, where an ambulance was parked. Light streamed from all the windows of the house and, although it was dusk, he had no difficulty in finding his way to the back garden.

Here he found Inspector Whitelaw and a scene of crime officer and his team, all awaiting instructions. Dr Band was even then making a preliminary examination of the body, and he emerged from the shed, shaking his head. As he did so the pathologist, Dr Ghent, appeared. He explained his relatively rapid arrival by the fact that he had been at the Carsons' place; he and David had been playing a round of golf together. He'd had no time for a cup of tea, he said plaintively, let alone a drink, when his damned bleeper—as he called it—went off and he had to get on the phone.

'Brigadier Carson?' Tansey asked sharply. 'Was there anyone else there?'

'Mrs Carson and the boy—their son, Alan.'

'And you told them why you'd been called away—that Major Aston had shot himself?'

'No—I—Of course not. I just said I'd been called to the Astons'. No more than that.'

Tansey noted the hesitation, and didn't believe him. He looked at Ghent in some disgust. 'Your version will be all over Coriston College tonight or tomorrow morning, whenever Alan goes back to school.'

'Does it really matter?' Band asked. 'There's bound to be gossip everywhere.'

'There's such a thing as discretion, especially in the early stages of an inquiry,' Tansey said. He was not prepared to be tactful. 'Didn't Carson tell you he knew Aston?' he asked Ghent. 'Wasn't he shocked?'

'Of course he was shocked.' The pathologist hesitated, realizing that he had tacitly admitted Tansey's earlier accusation of indiscretion. 'Carson said he'd had a drink with Aston this morning after the church parade and Aston had seemed in surprisingly good form, considering this business of his daughter. Which reminds me. Post-mortem on Hannah tomorrow at nine sharp. You'll be there, Chief Inspector?'

'I will.'

'Fine,' said Ghent. 'Now shall we stop chewing the rag and get on with this one?'

Donning plastic overshoes and gloves, the two doctors, led by Tansey and Whitelaw, carefully entered the shed. By this time extra lighting had been set up outside to shine through the windows, and photographers were checking their equipment. Orderlies were waiting with the metal trolley on which Richard Aston's body would be removed to the ambulance and thence to the mortuary. Sergeant Donaldson and two police constables were standing by.

Major Aston's body was slumped over a bench, and his brains splattered the walls and the floor. An old service revolver was still gripped in his right hand, and its cleaning implements were carefully arranged around him. It was not a pretty sight.

Ghent took one look and said, 'Why call me? Your most junior constable could tell you the cause of death, and I gather one officer actually heard the shot.'

'That's true,' said Tansey. 'but we've got regulations, as you know quite well.'

'Seen enough?' asked Ghent. 'Can I turn the body? I assume you want to search the pockets.'

'Please,' said Tansey. 'At first sight, do you think the wound's compatible with the kind of old service revolver he's holding.'

'Sure,' said the pathologist. 'Why not? At that range, any weapon would do this sort of damage. I may be able to tell you more when I've had him on the table, but in the meantime all I can say is that if that's Aston, he's dead. There's both an entry and an exit wound. It's clear he shot himself, especially as your policeman was on the scene within seconds, but you'd have to be clairvoyant to know if it was an accident or on purpose. Myself, I'd plump for the latter, but don't quote me. As far as compatibility's concerned, it wasn't a shotgun, but any other weapon at that range could have done the same damage.'

'If it was on purpose,' said Band, who was always prepared to be helpful, 'the Major set the scene to look like an accident very carefully. Remembrance Sunday. He decides to clean what I would guess was his father's old World War One service revolver and—a moment's thoughtlessness . . . Moreover, he chooses the garden shed, not the house, and he knows there's a policeman on duty to cope. Very considerate of him, I'd say.'

'Yes,' said Tansey thoughtfully. He turned to Whitelaw. 'Get his pockets emptied before they take him away. Then a thorough search round here and later in the house. We've got to make sure about the note, if any. And we must find out where he kept the gun.' A thought occurred to him. 'What about Mrs Aston and her sister?' he asked.

'Mrs Aston's more or less collapsed,' said Whitelaw, 'but her sister, Mrs Turnbull, she's made of stern stuff. A very capable woman. She put Mrs Aston to bed and sent for Dr Fenwick who's their personal GP. She's giving the police every facility.'

'Fine,' said Tansey. 'I'll go and have a word with her. Thanks very much, and good night,' he said to the doctors. 'We'll get to work as soon as you're sure you've finished.'

'I'm finished now, till I see him at the PM,' said Ghent.

'And there's nothing more I can do,' said Band. 'Fenwick will look after the arrangements when the body's eventually released.'

The Chief Inspector went around to the front door of the house, accompanied by Sergeant Donaldson, and rang the bell.

'Mrs Turnbull?' he said, when the door was opened.

'Yes, I'm Priscilla Turnbull.' She led them into a sitting-room, moved some knitting and a spectacle case from her chair and turned to face them.

'Please sit down, Mrs Turnbull. I'm Chief Inspector Tansey, and this is Sergeant Donaldson. I'm sorry to disturb you, but I need to ask some questions.'

'You're not disturbing me, Chief Inspector. I'm just trying to keep myself occupied.' Priscilla motioned the two officers to chairs. 'What is it you want to know? I'll tell you whatever I can, though you can probably answer my questions better than I can answer yours.'

'First, how's Mrs Aston?'

'She's asleep. Dr Fenwick came at once and gave her a strong sedative. He's going to look in again early tomorrow. It's been an appalling blow, this accident, coming on top of Hannah's death, but Irene's got a lot of courage. She'll be all right.'

'I'm glad,' Tansey said tactfully, and wondered what further blows were in store for Mrs Aston. He hesitated. 'Mrs Turnbull, I have to ask you. What sort of mood was Major Aston in? No one would have expected him to be on top of his form, but was he depressed because of the circumstances surrounding Hannah's death?'

Priscilla gave Tansey a shrewd glance. 'He was upset, naturally, but he was bearing up very well, I thought. Both Irene and I commented on his cheerfulness. She was the more "down" of the two, and I think he was making a big effort for her sake.' Priscilla went on to describe Richard Aston's description of his morning, and his demeanour over lunch. 'Chief Inspector, you're not implying this wasn't an accident, are you?'

'No, Mrs Turnbull. So far we've found nothing to suggest that it was other than accidental.'

'No note?' And when Tansey shook his head. 'How did it happen? I know he shot himself, but he'd been a soldier. He was used to guns.'

'People who are used to guns are often more careless than those who aren't.' Tansey stood up. 'Thank you for being so frank, Mrs Turnbull. But I'm afraid we'll have to impose on you further. A team will want to search the house—especially Major Aston's study, which they would like to do as soon as possible, and his bedroom—perhaps tomorrow, if Mrs Aston's recovered sufficiently. I shall also have to interview Mrs Aston when her doctor says I may. Now, I know this is a dreadful shock for both of you. Would you like a woman police officer to spend the night here with you?'

'Thank you, no. Inspector Whitelaw asked me that when he arrived and I refused.' Priscilla smiled. 'The police outside will be quite enough.'

'I'll say good night, then. If there's anything you need, please ask Inspector Whitelaw.'

Tansey gave a half bow. He had met women like Priscilla Turnbull before. He didn't understand them, but he respected them and, he admitted to himself, they were useful witnesses. With Sergeant Donaldson he went back to the garden.

Inspector Whitelaw was looking grim. One of the police officers was vomiting over Richard Aston's cauliflowers. Aston's remains, decently covered, were on the metal trolley and were being wheeled around to the front of the house and the waiting ambulance.

'A right mess!' Whitelaw said. 'Thank God for the women's sake he didn't do it in the house.'

'Have they found the round?'

'The round?'

'The bullet! The thing that killed him. It must have gone through his head and be embedded somewhere in that place. Find it and get forensic to match it with the gun, just for the record. And I assume there's no trace of a note?'

'No, sir. I'd have told you at once if we'd found one. OK. It could have been an accident. I accept the possibility. But why choose today of all days to clean his father's old revolver, if that's what it is? A sentimental gesture, maybe?' Whitelaw shook his head.

'Let's keep an open mind,' Tansey said, 'at least for the moment. Things aren't always as neat and obvious as one expects them to be, Inspector. If Richard Aston took his own life intentionally, the main question is why? Was it innocent grief at his beloved daughter's dreadful death, or could it possibly have been remorse for having done away with her himself? We're trying to find Hannah Aston's killer, remember. Don't let's blame Richard for it until we're sure, or someone else might get killed.'

Slightly surprised at his own tetchiness, Tansey said that he would be going straight to the PM on Hannah the next day, and would come to Colombury immediately afterwards. Then, having giving Whitelaw some instructions about the searches—instructions the Inspector did not really need—he said, 'Good night, and thank you all for your efforts.' Then he went around the side of the house to his car.

A man was standing at the top of the lane and, as he stepped outof the shadow of the trees, Tansey realized that he was not a police officer.

'Chief Inspector Tansey?'

'Yes. Who are you. What do you want?'

'Derek Lander. Press. Freelance.' He waved a card at Tansey, but it was too dark for the Chief Inspector to study it. 'Would you care to comment, sir?'

'What on?'

'Major Aston. He's shot himself, hasn't he? Did he leave an explanatory note?'

The two men had been standing near each other, but now Chief Inspector Tansey took a long stride forward so that they were almost touching. Tansey, by several inches the taller, glared down at Lander. He saw that Lander was young, and realized that he could only be a cub reporter out to get his name in print. But Tansey wanted to know the man's source. The most likely, due to Ghent's indiscretions, were the Carsons, but he had to try to make sure.

'Who the hell told you Major Aston had shot himself?'

Lander was taken aback by this unexpected display of antagonism. 'I—er,' he stammered. 'I have my sources.'

'In the police?'

'No, no! A stringer.'

'A stringer? You?' Tansey snorted with laughter. 'Laddie, people like you don't have stringers. You *are* stringers. But someone called you. Who?'

'I can't tell you, Chief Inspector. You know that. Sources are privileged.'

'Until you get to court, Mr Lander, and face a contempt

charge. Meanwhile, I'll have you arrested. Acting suspiciously at the scene of a death will do. We can hold you for thirty-six hours without a charge, and they could be thirty-six uncomfortable hours.'

'But I've done nothing.'

'You're withholding from the police information that could be vital to a murder investigation. Now, be sensible, Lander. Who tipped you off about Major Aston?'

'OK,' Lander said reluctantly. 'It was Alan Carson, Brigadier Carson's son. He's only a kid and he doesn't need the money, which isn't much anyway, but it makes him feel important to consider himself in touch with the media, and he does come up with items from time to time.'

'Such as tonight. An overheard confidence to his father, a confidence that should never have been uttered.'

'You can't blame me for that, Chief Inspector. It's my job to get information where I can.'

'Sure. And what else has Alan Carson told you about the Astons?'

'He told me about Hannah's riding accident at the Drivers' place, which he said was her fault. That was a small scoop.' Lander was becoming sulky. 'And though it's no use to me, you might be interested in this titbit, Chief Inspector. He said he wasn't surprised Hannah got herself murdered. According to him, she was asking for it, leading guys on—guys like Rod Driver—and then, if they made the slightest response, blowing them away like—like shit.'

'I see.'

What the Chief Inspector saw was that Alan Carson was a trouble-maker. But the boy's assessment of Hannah as what was sometimes called a prick-teaser reinforced what Tansey had learnt from others. Whether or not this was deliberate on Hannah's part he didn't know, but he suspected that she had been a girl to whom men were involuntarily attracted, as cats are attracted to someone who fears and dislikes physical contact with them.

'And that's all Alan told me, Chief Inspector,' Lander continued, except that he believes Marjorie Eversley knows more about Hannah's love-life than she's let on so far.'

'What makes you and Carson so sure she had a "love-life"?' Tansey asked absently.

'Well, there's a rumour going round town that she was pregnant—'

'OK, Mr Lander.' Tansey sighed. He had had his fill of the reporter. 'In return for your help I'll give you some information, which should really come from our Press Office. Major Aston was cleaning an old revolver. He shot himself. No suicide note has been found. All indications at present are that it was an accident. Now, get out of here!'

'Thanks, Chief Inspector. Thanks a lot,' Lander said, and rapidly strode off down the lane.

Tansey followed more slowly; he had much to occupy his mind.

CHAPTER 18

'Coffee?' asked Dr Ghent.

'Please,' said Chief Inspector Tansey.

Although Tansey did not particularly like Ghent, he had no fault to find with his work. Watching, as was his legal duty, the pathologist dissect, examine and label all that remained of Hannah Aston, the detective had been forced to admire Ghent's deft skill. But he was thankful when the ordeal was over. Though he didn't consider himself squeamish, attending post-mortems was not a pastime he relished.

'Well, what can you tell me now?' he asked as an assistant in a white coat brought coffee into Ghent's office.

'A little more. Not too much at the moment.' Ghent never liked to commit himself immediately. 'But I can tell you the girl died of asphyxiation due to strangulation—which you've probably assumed already from the marks you saw on her neck. And she didn't die where she was found.'

He paused to sip some coffee, and Tansey said, rather acidly, 'I scarcely imagined she and her companion went for a swim in the quarry, fully dressed, and she got strangled under water.'

Ghent smiled wryly. 'You misunderstand me, Chief Inspector. What I'm trying to say is that Hannah was strangled in one place, and then transported in a confined space—possibly the boot of a small car—to the quarry. She was certainly dead when she entered the water.'

'She couldn't have gone voluntarily to the quarry and been killed there?' Tansey was regretting his earlier semi-facetious remark about swimming in the quarry. He knew that Ghent could be unhelpful if he were riled, and then information could be delayed or a reasoned suspicion not reported.

'No. Of course, rigor mortis had worn off under water, but there's evidence that her limbs had been constricted for some time after death.' Ghent went into some medical details which Tansey didn't entirely follow. 'But don't ask me for how long. I can't say. But if I'm right about the car, and you can find it, there should be at least some sign—hair, perhaps—to show she'd been shut up in the boot.'

'Did she put up a struggle against her assailant?'

'Yes, indeed. I was coming to that. There was skin tissue and specks of dried blood under her nails, which could condemn her killer, once you've identified him. I'll let you have the results as soon as I can.'

'Thanks,' said Tansey, thinking of the many cars owned

by the staff at Coriston and the Drivers' vehicles and the Mergers' and all the others that could have been borrowed. To examine every possibility would be an enormous task. But the blood specks could be useful immediately. Even if they turned out to be from the most common group they ought to help to eliminate some of the people who had been involved with Hannah. And of course later the new-fangled genetic fingerprinting would be invaluable with both the blood and the tissue samples—that was, if the process were still fashionable by the time the case came to trial.

'That's great!' he said. 'The sooner the better, needless to say. Just the simple blood group would help to start with.'

'Of course,' Ghent nodded his head in understanding. 'Now, there's one other thing of some importance. I gather you believed Hannah was pregnant?'

'*She* believed she was!'

'She was wrong. There's no sign that she was pregnant, or ever had been pregnant.'

'Well, I'm damned!' said Tansey. But there was no doubt that Hannah Aston had believed she was pregnant. It was the only reasonable explanation for her recent behaviour, the gin-drinking episode and the visit to the clinic. What was more, she had admitted the fact to her father—she had told him that she would rather die than have the baby—and she had convinced Richard Aston.

It crossed Tansey's mind that Hannah might have been somewhat unbalanced about sex; it would fit in with much of what he had been told about her. But he thrust these psychological speculations aside. 'I suppose she wasn't a virgin,' he said dubiously.

'Definitely not,' replied Ghent. 'I'd say she was used to intercourse. As to believing herself pregnant, that presents no problem. She was anæmic, and this could account for her missing a couple of periods. Then if she and the current boyfriend had failed to take precautions on some occasion, or an ex-lover or any boy she went out with had more or less raped her—"date rape", they call it nowadays, don't they?—she could easily have assumed the worst.'

'Quite!' This, Tansey thought, was the reverse of the coin: from Hannah the untouchable virgin you flip over to Hannah the good-time girl. It was impossible to accept either facet in its entirety.

'Let's get back to Hannah's death, shall we, Ghent?' he said. 'She was strangled, carried in an enclosed space—probably the boot of a car—and then, minus one shoe, thrown into the quarry. Had she had sex—rape or not—immediately before all this?'

'No-o, I don't think so. It's hard to tell after she'd been in the water, but certainly there are no obvious signs of forcible entry, though, as I said, she must have struggled with her assailant when she was attacked. However—'

'Go on!' Tansey was impatient. 'I won't sue you if you're wrong, and any guess might help to find her killer.'

'It's conceivable, but I wouldn't swear to it—indeed, I shan't put it in the report—but I suppose she might have been sexually assaulted after she was dead, or when she was unconscious and on the verge of death.'

Tansey nodded his thanks. 'Not a pretty picture,' he said, and thought that if Ghent were right the killer was perhaps a former lover whom she no longer wanted, or someone who felt he had been led on and then spurned. Peter Merger, in spite of his denials, seemed the most likely candidate in the first category, but in the second the field was wide open.

Ghent was looking at his watch. 'Chief Inspector, I don't want to hurry you, but that's all I can tell you at the moment. I'll let you have a full report as soon as I can.'

'Especially the initial details on the blood. They could be an enormous help right away, as I said,' Tansey replied.

'Will do,' Ghent promised. 'I'll let you have that without any delay.'

'Please,' Tansey said, thankful that the pathologist, perhaps mindful of his indiscretion at the Carsons' the previous evening, was being so cooperative.

He looked at his own watch. 'My sergeant's meeting me here in a few moments. May I leave my own car and pick it up later?'

'Of course,' said Ghent.

Tansey found Abbot waiting for him outside the mortuary, as he had arranged on the phone earlier that morning. As Abbot drove off, the Chief Inspector quickly briefed him on the previous day's developments and the results of the PM, and then reached for the phone to speak to Headquarters. Inspector Whitelaw had no further news for him. Nick Hayne had supposedly been sighted in London, but that had turned out to be a false alarm. In return Tansey passed on the information that Hannah had not been pregnant, and that the cause of her death was strangulation.

'There'll be more to come later,' he said. 'Meanwhile, I'm off to Colombury with Abbot. I must look in on Mrs Aston and her sister, and while I'm in the town there are one or two points I'd like to check on.'

He was purposely vague. Almost all that he proposed to do he could have left to Whitelaw or even Sergeant Donaldson and his officers. But this was to some extent a preliminary inquiry, which he hoped could be conducted without raising much interest among those concerned. A lot would depend on Dr Ghent's reports.

Abbot drove fast, and they reached the Astons' house in good time. Irene Aston was pale, her face blotched with weeping, but she was up and dressed and quite composed; she had even made an attempt to cover the signs of her distress with make-up. She insisted that the two police officers should have some coffee, and Priscilla went to make it.

'I feel as if I were living in a dream, or rather a nightmare,' Irene said honestly, 'but of course I'm not going to wake up. Chief Inspector, was Richard's death an accident? I hope and pray that it was. But—I want to know the truth.'

'Mrs Aston, all I can tell you is that there's no evidence to suggest that Major Aston deliberately took his own life. Of course he was unhappy, but from what we've learnt he appears to have been as cheerful as could be expected yesterday before his death.'

And that's the truth, Tansey thought, though it wasn't the whole truth. 'Incidentally, Mrs Aston, can you tell us anything about this service revolver your husband had in his possession?'

Irene nodded. 'It belonged to his father. Richard treasured it. He used to clean it every year, not—not always on Remembrance Sunday, and he was very careful with it. He kept it locked in a drawer of his desk in his little study. I didn't know he had any ammunition for it.'

Tansey said, 'Thank you. You've fully answered my question.'

They were interrupted by the return of Mrs Turnbull with the coffee and a plate of biscuits. Abbot got up and shut the door behind her. Unlike Tansey, who had had enough coffee with the pathologist, he eyed the tray with approval.

While Mrs Turnbull poured and Abbot passed around the cups and the biscuits, Tansey continued. 'I do have a little information about Hannah's death which I hope may be a slight comfort to you, Mrs Aston,' he said tentatively, thinking how incongruous the coffee party setting was for such a conversation. 'We know now that her death was quick, which was one good thing.'

'How did she die? Was she drowned?' Irene's voice was choked.

Tansey hesitated before replying. Then he said, 'No, she didn't drown, Mrs Aston. She was dead a while before she was put in the quarry. She was strangled.' The Chief Inspector saw Irene Aston wince, but there was no gentle way of telling her how her daughter had died, and it would be common knowledge at least at the time of the inquest. 'She didn't suffer, hardly at all. She had not been assaulted before her death. I hope that's a little consolation to you, Mrs Aston.'

'And thank God for it, Irene,' Priscilla said.

The Chief Inspector and Sergeant Abbot exchanged glances, and read each other's thoughts. They were not unkind men, but they had a job to do, and it was to their advantage that Mrs Turnbull was so balanced and bracing even if, had they themselves been in similar circumstances, they might not have appreciated her. Tansey had drunk his coffee quickly, and now he gave Abbot the briefest of nods. He turned to Irene Aston.

'As Mrs Turnbull will have told you, your house was searched yesterday evening, just in case the Major had left a farewell note in his study or somewhere else. I'm afraid these things have to be done, if only to satisfy the coroner.'

'Of course. I understand.'

'Naturally your bedroom was not searched at the time, as you were asleep there. Might we look through it now? And perhaps glance at your car, too?' he added, as if it were an afterthought.

'Yes—yes. I suppose so, though I can't imagine where—'

'I'll show them,' said Priscilla, standing up. 'The bedroom first?'

They followed Mrs Turnbull upstairs and, while she stood in the doorway, made a fairly thorough search of the bedroom which Richard and Irene Aston had shared. As expected, they did not find anything of interest. It was possible, Tansey knew, that Aston had left his wife a farewell note which she had found and destroyed to prevent his suicide becoming publicly known but, to judge from her behaviour, he thought that unlikely. He was much more interested in the Astons' car.

This, however, proved a disappointment. The Astons drove a six-year-old Ford, which they had bought second-hand. It had a variety of dents and scrapes, but was kept scrupulously clean outside. Inside, there was the usual paraphernalia that cars seemed to collect—maps, a box of tissues, a pair of driving gloves and a torch. Abbot opened the boot.

'You can't imagine Richard would leave a note in there, surely?' Priscilla Turnbull said.

The Chief Inspector didn't answer at once. He was staring into the boot in exasperation. It contained an old school raincoat, a scarf and some trainers. He could see a pale hair adhering to the scarf. But even if Richard Aston had killed his daughter and transported her in the back of his car, it would be impossible to prove from this evidence, since there was no reason why hairs from Hannah's head or her fingerprints should not be found there.

Swearing under his breath, Tansey banged shut the boot. It would be a waste of time to send the Astons' car to the forensic lab, and it was a waste of time lamenting the fact. In any case, Richard Aston might well not be guilty.

He turned to Priscilla Turnbull. 'Thank you very much, Mrs Turnbull. We'll just say goodbye to Mrs Aston, then we'll be off.'

'If you've seen all you want, Chief Inspector—' Priscilla looked at Tansey curiously, but didn't comment further.

And five minutes later the two officers had made their escape.

*

Once in the car Tansey reached for the phone again and, after a brief delay, got through to Dr Ghent at the path lab.

'Sorry to bother you again so soon,' he said, 'but there's something I need you to do. I should have thought of it before.' He explained quickly, wondered if he should warn Ghent to be discreet and decided against it.

The phone rang the instant he had replaced the receiver. Inspector Whitelaw was on the radio. He had two items of interest. A man answering to Nick Hayne's description had been taken into custody in Scotland, in the Trossachs. He had been sleeping rough, was ravenously hungry and said he was trying to escape from the devil. He had refused to give his name or say where he had come from. But he had admitted that he wanted his 'Gran'.

'We can have him if we want him, they say,' Whitelaw added. 'I think they want to get rid of him. And he does sound like our man, sir.'

'OK. We'll have him. But nothing dramatic—just 'wanted for questioning to help inquiries', as they say. Try to make arrangements for the Scots to take him to Glasgow or Edinburgh airport, and we'll send someone up on the shuttle from Heathrow to bring him back, and make sure he's treated well. He'll be here sometime tomorrow, I imagine.'

'I guess so, sir. I'll fix it.'

'Right.' Once again Tansey blessed Whitelaw's efficiency. 'You mentioned two items?'

'There's a letter for you. Posted yesterday in Colombury, marked "Private and Confidential", and addressed in handwriting—so it's probably not from an anonymous crank.'

Possibilities flicked rapidly through Tansey's mind, but he dismissed them. 'I'll be back in mid-afternoon,' he said. 'It'll keep till then.'

'Very good, sir,' said Whitelaw.

'And where to now, sir?' asked Abbot.

'A quick sandwich,' said Tansey. 'Then off to Coriston. We're going to make inquiries about motor vehicles as tactfully as possible. I'm hoping Dr Sheringham's secretary will be able to help. But while you're driving us to the Windrush Arms—they must know us there by now—I'm going to use the phone yet again.'

As he spoke Tansey was looking up numbers in his notebook. He tried the Drivers' and was answered by a man's voice he didn't recognize. 'Colombury Riding School.'

'Hello,' said Tansey. 'Who's that?'

'Stan Monk. I'm the stable lad. The Drivers aren't here at present. Who are you? Can I help?'

'Police,' said Tansey, 'checking up on a vehicle. What do they have at the school? A horsebox, I suppose, and—'

'Sure, a horsebox and a Land-Rover, and Mrs Driver usually uses a Mini.'

Tansey had seen these for himself in the yard, and knew that none of them were really suitable for transporting a concealed body. The Land Rover had no boot and big windows, the Mini was too small and no one was likely to drive up to the quarry with a horsebox. 'Nothing else?' he asked.

'No. I have a motorbike myself. Why?'

'Just looking for a Toyota that witnessed an accident the other day. Thanks for your help.'

He put down the receiver. He had been lucky to get the stable lad and not one of the Drivers. He didn't think he could try the same trick with the Mergers. Anyway, he already knew that Peter drove a Fiat, in which he claimed to have spent the night when Hannah disappeared; inquiries had produced no witnesses to this, though the Fiat had been seen earlier outside the Fanshawes' house in Shipton.

'Here we are, sir,' said Abbot, turning into the car park of the Windrush Arms.

As promised, the Chief Inspector arrived back at HQ in mid-afternoon. The visit to Coriston had been comparatively successful. Dr Sheringham's secretary had explained that there was a limited number of garages available to the school. Housemasters and one or two others, such as the Chaplain, had priority, but otherwise it was a matter of length of service. Those who had no garages parked their cars in marked and numbered spaces to one side of School House. And, yes, she had an alphabetical list, from which Abbot took quick notes while Tansey asked about the garaged cars. He learnt that the Brownes had an old Volvo station wagon and a nearly new Fiesta. The only disappointment was that several cars in the parking places were unlocked, and many had keys in their ignitions. They could easily have been borrowed.

Wondering if he had wasted his own and Abbot's time, Tansey went into his office. At once he saw the letter, which Whitelaw had placed in the centre of his desk. He hadn't forgotten about it, but it had not been in the forefront of his mind. He found a pair of thin gloves in a drawer, slit open the envelope and carefully extracted a sheet of plain grey notepaper. The handwriting meant nothing to him, and he turned at once to the signature.

The letter was signed 'Richard Aston'.

CHAPTER 19

Detective Chief Inspector Tansey read the letter with a mixture of revulsion and pity and for minutes afterwards he sat, staring at the sheet of notepaper and the precise italicized handwriting. He would have to refer it to the Chief Constable, but first he wanted to be clear in his mind how much of it he believed to be the truth. Slowly, trying to analyse it objectively, he read the letter for a second time.

Dear Chief Inspector,

When you get this I shall be dead. I propose to shoot myself. I should have done this a long time ago for the sake of Irene and Hannah—especially Hannah—but I have always been a self-indulgent man.

Hannah's death has appalled me. I know that I was responsible, though I did not actually kill her. Later, I will explain what I believe may have happened. But first I must tell you that I have had sexual intercourse with Hannah, my own daughter, since she was ten years old.

It came about naturally and, on her part, perfectly innocently. Irene had gone into hospital to have a hysterectomy, and Hannah, frightened by a nightmare, crept into my bed.

After the operation Irene was not too well for a while, and she had no desire for sex. At the time, I was stationed in Germany, and I acquired a mistress, a German girl who worked in the officers' mess, but I still took Hannah from time to time. Then we returned to England, and subsequently retired to Colombury. By now Hannah no longer wanted me. She appreciated the full moral, legal and social significance of what we had been doing, but I was her father, in a position of authority. I insisted and she couldn't easily refuse. I admit I was selfish, thinking only of my own needs, but I did not ask her to satisfy me often. And I was always careful, which is why I could not understand how she could be pregnant. I accused her of having a lover, but she denied it vehemently, and I believed her. She said she never wanted to have sex with anyone ever—that I had spoiled it for her for always, that she hated even being kissed or touched, and it was all my fault. She was very angry—and with every reason. Abusing her was bad enough, God knows, but to make her pregnant

Anyway, apart from outside the Coriston School House before the Hallowe'en party, I never saw her again alive, but I think I know what happened. I think that to spite me, because of her anger at the accusation I had made, she played up to one of the masters or one of the senior boys, but at the last moment refused him, so that he killed her out of frustration. That is what I meant by saying I was responsible for Hannah's death. But I repeat, I swear to God that I did not actually kill her, and you must discover who did because he may kill some other girl. But as far as Hannah is concerned the blame is mine, and there is only one way out.

I waited until Priscilla had arrived. She will see Irene through and, though I have no right, I ask the authorities to make it as easy as possible for them.

Richard Aston.

Tansey folded the letter, returned it to its envelope and took off his gloves. Fifteen minutes later he was sitting in the Chief Constable's office, facing Midvale across his desk. He had briefly outlined what he had learnt from the pathologist that morning, and the Chief Constable was now studying Major Aston's letter.

'Nasty,' he said as he finished reading. 'Poor Hannah! Poor child! No wonder she disliked any physical contact or show of affection, even from her peers. This explains a lot about her, doesn't it?'

'Yes, it does indeed, sir, including why she couldn't face the thought of her mother knowing she was pregnant and demanding to get the name of the father.'

'What do you think of Major Aston's theory about the circumstances of her death?'

'It's a strong possibility, I suppose, that she was killed as a result of frustrated sex, but I do have reservations, sir. I can't visualize her throwing herself at someone just to spite her father. It strikes me as being out of character. I think it far more likely that someone made a pass at her believing it would be welcome, and then found it wasn't. And there's no reason why her killer was necessarily connected with Coriston. For instance, we're pretty sure Nick Hayne was in the College grounds on Hallowe'en, and he need not have been the only interloper.'

'No. By his own admission Aston himself was on the scene for some time, and once he supposed she was pregnant he certainly had a motive. But it would be pointless to lie in this letter about killing her, and yet admit to incest. Don't you agree?'

'Yes, I do, sir. I don't believe he killed her, but we'll know for sure before long. I asked Dr Ghent to compare the Major's genetic make-up with the tissue found under Hannah's nails. What's more, we may get a quick and simple answer from the blood groups.'

'Of course! It's a pity we can't do that with all potential suspects, but think what an outcry there'd be about the rights of the citizen in a free country.' Midvale's heavy face creased into a grin.

Tansey returned a wry smile. 'In fact, sir, it would save a lot of innocent people a lot of harassment.'

'Try telling that to the general public,' said Midvale and, suddenly grim, added, 'Chief Inspector, for the moment I'm going to put this letter in my safe, and its contents are strictly between us. We'll wait for Dr Ghent's verdict, and act accordingly. Until then the media can go hungry for juicy gossip.'

'Right, sir,' said Tansey. 'I'll let you know as soon as I

hear from Ghent. He promised to be as quick as he could.'

In the event the pathologist did not contact Tansey until late that day. He apologized for the delay. His report, he said, would be delivered by hand before noon the next morning, though the tissue typing the Chief Inspector had requested would take a few days. In the meantime, Tansey might be interested to know that the blood groups of Aston and his daughter were quite different, and that the specks of blood from under Hannah's nails did not match Aston's. It had also been confirmed that Hannah had been anæmic. What Ghent couldn't understand was why the stupid girl hadn't told her mother of her fears and gone to a doctor. The Chief Inspector didn't enlighten him.

Tansey passed on the news to the Chief Constable, and to Inspector Whitelaw, who received it without much enthusiasm; Whitelaw's only comment was that at least it narrowed the field of suspects by one.

Nick Hayne was escorted to the Headquarters of the Thames Valley Police early in the afternoon of the following day by the plain-clothes officer who had brought him from Scotland. Sergeant Abbot met them at the entrance, and took Nick to Chief Inspector Tansey's office at once. He joked with him on the way. It had already been decided that it would be best to treat the young man in a friendly fashion, as if he were not under any suspicion, but was merely being asked to volunteer information.

'Hello, Nick. Come along in,' said Tansey. 'You don't mind if I call you Nick, do you? I'm Chief Inspector Tansey.'

'No, no. Everybody calls me Nick. Hello, Chief Inspector. I saw you once before in Mergers' in Colombury. You must know Sergeant Donaldson. I don't like him. He's not a kind man, not like old Sergeant Court.'

Nick Hayne leant across the Chief Inspector's desk and

offered his hand, which Tansey shook. Nick them lumbered across to Sergeant Abbot and shook hands with him, as he had done on his arrival at HQ. After which, apparently satisfied, he seated himself in the chair Tansey had indicated.

At least this display had given Tansey a moment to appreciate that Nick's large and pleasant face had been badly scratched, though the scratches were healing. 'Have they given you any lunch, Nick?' he asked.

'Oh yes. Lovely. Up in the sky. You'd never think they could cook up there, would you, Chief Inspector? But I expect you know all about it. For me, this was the first time I've ever been in an aeroplane. It was smashing.'

Nick was voluble, and clearly over-excited by his day's experiences. Tansey let him talk. Nick was so childlike and forthcoming that it was difficult to think of him as an adult. But in physique he was a big and powerful man, and Tansey had noted the strength of his hands. Hannah Aston would have stood no chance against him.

At last Nick appeared to have no more to say. He smiled broadly from Tansey to Abbot and relaxed in his seat, waiting on them.

'Nick,' Tansey said, 'we want you to help us.'

'All right, as long as I can go home to Gran afterwards.'

Tansey nodded. 'First of all, you remember the Hallowe'en party at Coriston College, don't you? You dressed up in a sheet, and went as a ghost.'

Nick frowned. 'I shouldn't have taken Mrs Maple's sheet, I know. Gran was angry with me. She said it was stealing. But I didn't want to make holes in one of Gran's sheets. She'd have been even angrier if I'd done that.'

Abbot smothered a laugh at this ingenuous comment, and Tansey had to suppress a grin. But he was pleased that Nick had admitted without reservation to being at Coriston on Hallowe'en; so far Nick seemed to be doing his best to cooperate.

'Did you enjoy the party?' Tansey asked. 'Did you go into the disco?'

'No, I didn't. I stayed outside, but I could hear the music and it was fine until—'

'Until what, Nick?'

'I can't tell you that. I can't.' Nick had suddenly become very agitated. 'I was scared. I knew I ought not to be there. It's a dangerous time, Hallowe'en. There are all sorts of evil spirits around, real ones, not pretend ones like me, and if they think you've spied on them they'll punish you later.'

'What did you do when you were scared?' Tansey inquired, skirting the subject of what had frightened Nick.

'I bolted. I wanted to go home, back to Gran. I knew I'd be safe with Gran.'

'Did you take a car, Nick? You do drive, don't you?'

'Yes, I can drive, but I don't have a car, or a licence. I don't understand, Chief Inspector. I didn't steal a car, if that's what you mean. I didn't need a car. I had my bike. I'd hidden it at the end of the drive by the gate.'

In his agitation Nick was feeling in his jacket. Whatever he was seeking seemed to have slipped through a hole in his pocket and embedded itself in the bottom of the lining, where it eluded him. He stood up, as if thereby to reach it more easily. He was no longer listening to Tansey.

Tansey exchanged glances with Abbot, then saw the Sergeant's expression change. Abbot's eyes widened, his mouth opened slightly and he appeared to take a deep breath. He was staring past Tansey at Nick Hayne.

Nick had retrieved whatever he had been searching for, and was regarding with a satisfied smile a rectangular object studded with bright pieces of coloured glass. It was the missing buckle from Hannah Aston's witch's shoe but, as Nick played with it, moving it so that the light from the window was reflected on different facets of the glass, Tansey couldn't believe that the man was aware of its significance.

'That's pretty, Nick,' he said at last, keeping his voice light. 'Do you know what it is?'

'It's like a brooch, but I don't see how you fix it on.' Nick frowned, puzzled.

'I think it's a buckle off a shoe,' said Tansey, casually holding out his hand. 'Where did you get it, Nick?'

Nick thrust the buckle back into his pocket. 'I found it.' He looked at Tansey suspiciously. 'I didn't steal it, Chief Inspector. I found it that night I was at Coriston. It was on the ground among the grass. It's mine now.'

'That's not exactly true, Nick. If you find something you're meant to hand it in to the police and, if no one claims it as theirs after a certain amount of time, it's returned to you.'

'I didn't know that.' Nick was clearly disappointed. 'I have to give it to you?'

'We'll see. Nick, was that the night you scratched your face so badly?'

'No. I had my face covered with the sheet. I couldn't have scratched it then. I got the scratches up in the woods, before I went to Scotland.'

'What made you go to Scotland?'

'Because that's where the lorry was going. I got a lift. I couldn't stay in the woods, could I? And I had to get away from Sergeant Donaldson. He wanted to search our house but Gran wouldn't let him, though he'd only have found Mrs Maple's sheet. He told Gran he's be back with a warrant, and he'd have forced me to tell him about—about—'

Tansey held his breath but Nick, who had started to fidget in his chair, didn't continue, and the Chief Inspector wondered what he should do next. The evidence against Nick Hayne was mounting. Admittedly, it was all circumstantial, and Nick was not a fully responsible individual, but the facts couldn't be ignored. Nick had had the opportunity, the means and probably a motive for killing Hannah Aston; interrogated brutally—Tansey mentally shunned the word—Nick might confess, even though he was not guilty. On the other hand, the immediate question was whether Tansey's evidence and suspicions were sufficient to demand a warning before any further questioning. The Rules in the 1984 Act were very specific on such a point.

Nick temporarily solved the Chief Inspector's problem. 'I want to pee,' he said.

'OK,' Tansey said. 'Sergeant Abbot will show you the way.'

By the time they returned Tansey had made up his mind. He would avoid a warning for the moment. Before going any further Nick must be persuaded to explain why he had been so frightened at Coriston on Hallowe'en. If kindness didn't produce the answer, perhaps shock tactics would.

'Now, Nick,' he said as the young man resumed his seat. 'You remember you agreed to help us. So tell us about Hannah Aston.'

'I—I can't.'

'You'd rather tell Sergeant Donaldson?'

'No! No! But if I tell you he'll never bring her back. Don't you understand that, Chief Inspector? And he'll kill me or give me some dreadful disease. Gran too, perhaps. Don't ask me, please.'

For a moment Tansey was nonplussed. How on earth could Nick imagine that Donaldson could spread disease? Then, he realized what Nick meant.

'Nick,' he said, 'he—whoever he is—can't bring her back. Hannah's dead.'

'Dead? Oh, poor Hannah! Poor Hannah!'

There was no mistaking Nick's sincerity as he echoed the Chief Constable's words, and Tansey looked at him in exasperation. It was impossible to believe he was acting. The only alternative to his innocence was that he had blotted from his mind what he had done—a psychological concept that Tansey refused to accept.

'Listen to me,' said Tansey. 'This is important, Nick. If you tell us what you saw at Hallowe'en, you and your Gran will be quite safe. We'll protect you. I promise.'

'But you can't. You can't. Not against the Devil!'

'The devil? You mean someone dressed as a devil, like you were a ghost?'

'No! This was the Devil himself. He had horns and a tail and glittering eyes. His eyes were terrible, all shining, and his hands were covered with blood.'

Nick shuddered at the memory, and Tansey knew it was useless to argue with him. Nick was convinced he had seen the Devil and nothing would move him. As to his description, its accuracy had to be doubted, but 'How big was he?' Tansey asked. 'As big as you?'

'Not as big, no.' Nick said. Now he had taken the first step he was ready to talk. 'But he must have been strong. He was carrying this witch. I didn't know then that it was Hannah Aston. She had grey hair. Perhaps he'd already changed her into a hag. It was only the next day when they said Hannah had disappeared that I knew what had happened to her—that the Devil had taken her.' He shook his head sadly. 'I hoped he would bring her back, but you say she's dead.'

'Yes, Nick. I'm afraid so.'

'And you believe you can keep us safe, Chief Inspector, me and Gran.'

'I'm sure of it, Nick. The Devil—'

Tansey stopped abruptly as the phone rang. He restrained his irritation as he picked up the receiver. He had given strict instructions that he was not to be disturbed.

His caller was Inspector Whitelaw. 'Sir, I'm sorry to

interrupt you, but I thought you should know at once. Marjorie Eversley has been attacked at Coriston. Someone's tried to strangle her.'

CHAPTER 20

As soon as Mrs Eversley was informed that her daughter had been attacked, she drove at a furious pace to Coriston College, ignoring all speed limits. She found Marjorie lying fully dressed on a bed in the school sanatorium, having just been examined by Dr Fenwick, while Matron and an anxious Shirley Browne stood by.

'How is she?' Mary Eversley demanded immediately, staring at her daughter's white face. 'What happened?'

'She'll be all right,' said Fenwick. 'She's not hurt at all, except for some slight bruising on her throat. But I think it would be a good idea if she spent the night here. It'll help her recover from the shock.'

'Certainly not.' Mrs Eversley was determined. 'This place is obviously no longer safe. If you say she's not able to be moved I'll get another opinion—'

'She can be moved,' said Fenwick. 'I'll give you a sedative for her to take tonight.' He reached for his bag.

'Fine,' said Mary Eversley. 'In that case, she's leaving the school with me at once, and she's not coming back again. And now, will somebody please tell me what happened?'

'Mrs Eversley,' Shirley Browne said. 'We don't know yet. One of the gardeners heard what he thought was a cry and he discovered Marjorie lying on the ground in the shrubbery. Clearly she'd been attacked—look at the marks on her throat Dr Fenwick mentioned. But heaven knows what she was doing there at that time of day. She should have been in her form room.'

Marjorie spoke for the first time. 'Alan. Alan Carson,' she managed to croak.

She was shaken and her throat hurt. It had been a terrifying experience. When the hands had first clasped around her windpipe she had thought it was Alan playing some stupid joke, but as the fingers tightened and she had difficulty in breathing she knew this was no joke. What saved her was her presence of mind, and a memory.

She had read in a newspaper an article relating to Hannah's death which said that if someone was attempting to strangle you it was useless to try to pull the hands away, much better to go for his face or his genitals. So, reaching behind her, she had squeezed her attacker's balls with all the power that remained in her fingers and she thought that she had managed to utter a cry, even as a curtain of darkness came down over her eyes.

The next thing she remembered—and it could only have been moments later—was a couple of gardeners bending over her and one of them saying, 'Are you all right, lass?' She hadn't seen her assailant.

However, now that she was the centre of attention and with her mother beside her, she felt safe and rather proud of herself, as indeed she had reason to be. 'Alan Carson,' she said again, her voice a little clearer. 'I went to meet Alan.'

'Darling, don't try to talk.' Mary Eversley was helping her daughter to stand up and, as Marjorie shivered, pulled a blanket from the bed and wrapped it around her. 'Come along. There's nothing to worry about any more. We're going home and you're never coming to this dreadful place again.'

But Shirley Browne was persistent. 'Marjorie, are you saying it was Alan who attacked you?'

'No.' Marjorie shook her head. 'Don't know who it was,' she said shortly. 'But I went to the shrubbery to meet Alan.'

Hampered by the blanket she reached into the pocket of her skirt and extracted a piece of paper, which she passed to Shirley.

'Really, Mrs Browne.' Mary Eversley waved Shirley aside and, ignoring Dr Fenwick and Matron, led Marjorie from the room. 'My husband will be writing to Dr Sheringham,' she said over her shoulder.

'I didn't write that damned note, I tell you!'

'Carson!'

Alan Carson glared at Dr Sheringham. He was close to tears, and didn't care about the Headmaster's anger.

It was some while later and, together with Chief Inspector Tansey and Lance Condor, Carson's Housemaster, they were in the Headmaster's study. Shirley Browne had taken the note that Marjorie Eversley had given her directly to Dr Sheringham, with the information that Mrs Eversley had removed her daughter from the school. The news had not cheered Sheringham; in the course of the last week he had received phone calls from two of the College's governors complaining about the adverse publicity that Coriston had been receiving recently, and several calls from parents anxious for their children's safety.

'Why should I have written the note?' Alan demanded. 'There would have been no point. I had a double period of French after lunch today, and I was there in class. You can check.'

'That's true,' Condor said suddenly. 'I have already checked. Whoever it was in the shrubbery with Marjorie this afternoon it wasn't Alan.'

Alan threw him a grateful glance. 'And, please, I did not write that note. I know it looks like my handwriting, but can't they be compared?'

It was Tansey who answered. 'I doubt if that will be necessary. I accept that you didn't write the note, Alan, but I believe you may well have caused it to be written.'

'What do you mean by that?'

'Does the name Derek Lander mean anything to you?'

'No. Yes. He's a reporter, freelance. But what—'

'What has he got to do with you? It was he who told me that from time to time you passed on to him items of news, mainly gossip, usually about Coriston. Among these was the titbit that Marjorie Eversley was Hannah Aston confidante, and knew more about Hannah's love life than she had admitted. He wasn't the only person to whom you imparted this gem of information, was he?'

'I—I might have mentioned it.'

'Sure, Alan. You mentioned it, and the man who killed Hannah decided that Marjorie might put him at risk, and she must be eliminated too. Fortunately he didn't succeed.'

For a minute there was a strange silence in the room. Alan Carson was biting his lower lip. It was a harsh lesson, Tansey thought, but one that Alan deserved; he wouldn't invent or pass on gossip so carelessly in future. On the other hand, Tansey knew that he had reason to be grateful to the boy for forcing the killer into action.

'Chief Inspector!' Dr Sheringham was frowning fiercely. 'This is surmise on your part, isn't it? You can't know that that's what happened.'

'It's a reasoned guess, sir.'

'It implies that a member of this College was responsible.'

'Not necessarily, sir. Apart from Derek Lander, who else outside the school might you have told, Alan?' Tansey wished he could have asked Alan some more direct questions, but this was difficult in front of the Headmaster. He couldn't suggest names. 'People connected with Hannah,' he added.

'I told Rod Driver when I was out riding with him last Saturday, and he said he doubted if Hannah had any love life. She was a—"a cold little bitch" in his opinion.'

'Really, Alan!' Dr Sheringham was angry. 'Chief Inspector, I must protest. It's unfair to ask Alan to name names. He'll be mentioning masters next.'

This was rather what Tansey had hoped for, but he couldn't say so. Out of the corner of his eye he saw Lance Condor put a hand over his mouth as if to wipe away a grin. Hannah hadn't been in his House, he had never taught her or had any connection with her; he didn't feel under any suspicion. He could afford to be amused.

Tansey said, 'Dr Sheringham, I don't think Alan can help us any more, at least for the moment. But I would like to consult your secretary. She'll have a record of everyone's timetable in her computer, I imagine?'

'Yes,' Sheringham nodded. 'Anything else, Chief Inspector?'

'It's a little unusual, but I think it's justified by the large number of people involved. I'd like all the staff and students of Browne's House and Condor's House, plus anyone else who taught Hannah—say games or dancing or anything—to be assembled at a time convenient to you this evening. I believe, sir, that some of them may have helpful information of which they may be unaware.'

Sheringham looked surprised, but he didn't demur. 'Very good, Chief Inspector,' he replied. 'I'll arrange it. But I can't countenance any—any pressures, if you know what I mean.'

'I assure you I'll be tactful, sir.'

The Headmaster sighed. He was feeling old. He decided he would offer the governors his resignation to take effect at the end of the school year. That is, he reflected, if they didn't insist that he resigned his post before then.

*

By the time Browne's and Condor's had been assembled in School House that evening, Chief Inspector Tansey had acquired considerably more information. That it was largely negative was unimportant.

A fingertip search of the shrubbery had produced nothing, but this was not unexpected. The incredibly complicated timetable of the school's activities had been more interesting, as Tansey was led through its intricacies by the Headmaster's secretary. The attack on Marjorie could be timed within precise limits; the two gardeners had been interviewed by Inspector Whitelaw, and had proved to be sensible men, who made sensible statements. And from this evidence it was indisputable that Alan Carson, as he had maintained, was in the clear. However, of those most closely associated with Hannah, Ian Merger had had a free period, as had Stanley Tranter and the two masters, Browne and Blondel.

Sergeant Abbot had also been busy and had learnt some interesting facts. Left in Colombury by the Chief Inspector, he had gone at once to the Mergers' shop. Tansey was in no doubt that Alan Carson had confided in his friend Ian Merger his belief that Marjorie knew more about Hannah than she had admitted, and the likelihood was that Ian had passed on this information to his brother.

Abbot had found Rose Merger serving in the shop, which was unusual for her these days unless they were particularly busy, but he only had to wait for one customer to be served.

'Hello, Mrs Merger,' he said cheerfully. 'Where are all your menfolk?'

'Stocktaking. They've been at it since eight this morning, with a couple of half-hour breaks. They'll be dead tired tonight. It's heavy work moving all those crates and cases, but it has to be done if we're to be sure of what's needed for Christmas.'

'Can I go and have a word with them?'

'Why not? They'll be glad of an excuse to stop for a minute or two.'

Abbot found the two Mergers, father and son, in one of the two rooms behind the shop that were used as warehouses. With them was Ron Stewart, the warehouseman, who immediately seized his chance, sat on a crate and lit a cigarette.

'Don't tell me it's bad for my health, Alex Merger,' he said. 'You've been puffing more than I have.'

Alex Merger laughed. 'OK, Ron. Five minutes' break while we see what we can do for Sergeant Abbot.'

'Five minutes,' Abbot promised. 'What other time have you had off today?'

'Half an hour at ten and half at one o'clock,' said Alex promptly. 'We'll have another about four, then go on till we've finished the job. 'If only we had more space it wouldn't take so long, but—'

'Dad!' Peter interrupted. 'This isn't a social call. What is it you want, Sergeant?'

'To know if the three of you have been here all the afternoon,' said Abbot. He didn't blame Peter for his intervention.

'All day, except for our breaks, and even then we were together,' Alex said.

'Cast iron alibis, the three of us,' said Ron Stewart. 'Come clean, Bill. What's happened?'

He could see no reason not to tell them, and thoughtfully made his escape. He was glad Peter Merger was in the clear. About Rodney Driver he had no feelings one way or the other. But in the event Driver too had an unbreakable alibi. As Abbot arrived at the riding school in a car borrowed from Colombury police station, Driver rode into the yard with a couple of horsewomen, one of whom answered Abbot's query before it was asked.

'If that's what hunting entails,' she said in a loud, carrying voice. 'I think I'll stick to hacking. Three hours of your company may be delightful, Rod, but I'm going to be stiff as hell in the morning.'

And Abbot, making the spurious excuse that he was passing and thought he would inquire if the Drivers might be interested in buying a pony that he had heard of, drove on to Coriston and reported to Chief Inspector Tansey.

Tansey was pleased but not surprised at what Abbot had to say. In his own mind, he had reached the conclusion that Hannah Aston's killer and Marjorie Eversley's attacker was a member of Coriston College, and he was fairly sure who it was.

Proof was a different matter. But the killer had made a mistake in attacking Marjorie Eversley, an ill-considered mistake; it implied fear, panic and, what was more, it had provided a convenient way of narrowing the field of suspects. So there was a good chance that if the pressure could be increased the murderer would make another error—and perhaps this time a fatal one.

Tansey stood on the daïs at the end of the Assembly Hall in School House and looked down at the sea of young faces gathered there, together with a collection of their teachers, some of whom he had never seen before. Behind him sat Dr Sheringham and Sergeant Abbot, notebook open. The Headmaster had introduced him, and stated that all his questions must be answered and every assistance given to him; if this meant admitting to having broken a school rule, the offence would not be punished.

Tansey opened the proceedings. 'First, I'd like to ask you to cast your minds back to Hallowe'en,' he said, hoping he sounded more authoritative than he felt. 'It was the night that Hannah Aston disappeared. Hannah, as you must all know by now, was dressed as a witch. She wasn't the only witch, but some of you must have recognized her. Who danced with her? Who saw her leave the disco? Think!'

At first the answers came reluctantly, but after Morgan Browne admitted that he had danced with Hannah there was a spate of comments. None of them were very helpful. None of them added to what Tansey already knew. But two girls said they thought they might have seen Hannah leave the hall with someone dressed as a devil.

'That's interesting,' Tansey said, 'extremely interesting, and it tallies with some other information I have. Now, it was hot and noisy in the disco, and some of you went outside. I want to know if anyone who hasn't already told me about it saw a ghost—or a devil—while they were in the grounds.'

There was a shuffling of feet, and one or two coughs, but this merely served to accentuate the heavy silence that had followed these last questions. This was as far as he could go for the moment, Tansey decided. Perhaps it had been too far. No one moved.

Then, smiling, Beth Price stood up and solved the problem. An audible sigh of relief wafted through the hall; no one could suspect the young, attractive games mistress. 'I went out for a breath of fresh air,' she said. 'Incidentally, I was a ghost if anyone saw me, and I saw a devil, Mr Browne. He'd taken off his mask and seemed to be sneezing into it. I thought of offering him a handkerchief, but he went off towards his House. I should add that he was alone.'

'Thank you, Miss Price,' said Tansey, when the nervous laughter she had provoked had subsided, and thought that this at least partially confirmed Browne's story. 'Who's next?'

A games master, who gave his name as Saunders, said he had gone outside for a smoke. He had seen a large 'ghost' who had disappeared into the shrubbery, and a 'devil', whom he had taken for Mr Blondel because he had been near Blondel's car which was at the end of the row of parked vehicles. But on following him into the cloakroom he had found he had been wrong; this 'devil' was Stanley Tranter.

'You're sure they were one and the same devil?' Tansey asked. 'There seem to have been a lot around that night.'

'There certainly were,' said Saunders. 'It's a relatively simple costume. But no, Chief Inspector, I couldn't swear that the two I saw were one and the same man.'

When no one else volunteered any information, the Chief Inspector said he had no more questions, but he would like all those who had dressed up as devils to stay behind. The rest he thanked for their help.

From Nick Hayne's description, interpreted realistically, and from what he knew of Hannah Aston, Tansey had a fairly clear idea of the 'devil' he wanted. But more men—mainly masters—stayed behind than he had expected, and he had to spend some time whittling the numbers down even further. To his relief Dr Sheringham had retired, so that he could become less cautious, and exert more pressure, making even the innocent apprehensive. In the end he was left with five masters, two sixth form boys and Shirley Browne who, forgetting their previous quarrels, had refused to leave her husband.

'I have a request to make,' Tansey said, purposely ominous. 'In fact, it's more than a request, because if you don't do as I ask, I shall seek search warrants.'

There was a tremor in the room, as the law began to show its teeth, and the atmosphere was tense, which was Tansey's aim.

'What is it, Chief Inspector?' someone said.

'I would like each of you to bring me the suit he wore to the Hallowe'en party, and his devil's accoutrements, whatever they were—headgear, mask, tail or anything else. This material is required for forensic examination. Sergeant Abbot will help you to collect them.'

They stared at him, but they went; no one objected. And the Chief Inspector waited. The wait was an agony. He had set a trap for Hannah Aston's killer, but he knew it might not work. Because the man had panicked once, attacking Marjorie Eversley, it did not necessarily follow that he would panic now. Tansey could only hope.

The wait was not much easier for Inspector Whitelaw, who had been carefully briefed as to what he was to do. As soon as he saw Sergeant Abbot escorting the group from School House he had hurried, accompanied by a uniformed officer, to the line of parked cars at the side of the building.

Eventually, a figure carrying a bag approached at a fast walk, unlocked the end car, got in and tried to start it. It didn't start. Whitelaw had removed the distributor. Now he opened the driver's door.

'Sir, we have impounded your car for detailed examination, and I must ask you to come with me to Headquarters to help us with our inquiries into the death of Hannah Aston,' he said.

Stephen Blondel didn't speak. Slowly he got out of the car and handed the Inspector his bag. As he did so, the light caught his gold-rimmed spectacles and caused his eyes to appear to glitter. Later, in the hastily packed bag were found the horns and tail and the blood-red gloves he had worn at Hallowe'en. Nick Hayne's description of the devil he had seen carrying Hannah's body had not been inaccurate.

CHAPTER 21

A week later Detective Chief Inspector Tansey sat in the Chief Constable's office. Tansey had just left the inquest on Major Richard Aston.

'Well, how did it go?' Midvale asked.

'As expected, sir. An open verdict. It could hardly be otherwise without any suicide letter, could it?'

'No, indeed, and I'm sure it's for the best, even though it meant bending the law. In their separate ways both Aston and Hannah were tragic victims. Let them rest in peace. No one except the media would have gained from the true facts becoming known, and it would have ruined the rest of Mrs Aston's life.'

'She was at the inquest, sir, with Mrs Turnbull. I spoke to her at some length, and she said she was all right, but she couldn't bear Colombury any more. Too many memories. She's going to live with her sister.'

'I would think that was a good idea.'

'The Reverend Weston and his wife were at the inquest too, and I had quite a chat with them. Apparently the chap who takes care of the churchyard and does odd jobs is getting pretty old, and they're taking on Nick Hayne as an assistant. So things haven't turned out too badly for Nick, sir.'

'And we're left with Stephen Blondel. I must say, Chief Inspector, even now I don't really understand how you came to make him your primary suspect.'

'Well, sir, there were a number of pointers, some obvious, some less so. First, once we knew that Hannah's coat was still hanging in the cloakroom in the College, it seemed probable she'd been killed at Coriston, and improbable that someone unconnected with the place, such as Peter Merger or Rodney Driver, had put on fancy dress to go to this Hallowe'en party—though I kept an open mind about that for some time.

'Nick Hayne's "ghost" complicated matters, but in the end he did produce a valuable lead to a "devil". And of course there was Hannah's own character. She attracted men, possibly thanks to being abused over the years by her father, but didn't want them. Stephen Blondel seemed to me just the type of man who would be fascinated by her, as we now know from his confession that he was. He was rather shy and unsure of himself, and there was that incident when he was fairly new at Coriston and they were partners in some hare-and-hounds race. He saw this, quite wrongly, as a kind of bond between them, especially when they were ragged about it. Then, as her English master and her form master, he was closely involved with her, and he gave her extra coaching, which naturally she appreciated. But he failed to understand the girl.

'Anyway, confession apart, the scientific evidence in the boot of his car will be enough to convict him, though I believe him when he says he killed her accidentally in a fit of frustration. When they walked into the grounds together he thought she was encouraging him.

'Probably she was just being kind and he misunderstood. Men seem to have been attracted to her but, because of her relationship with her father, she wasn't able to deal with them as an ordinary girl would.'

'You may be right, Chief Inspector, but fortunately for us, that will be for a jury to decide. What do you suppose —manslaughter or unlawful killing?'

'I guess the former, sir. After all, his attack on Marjorie Eversley shows that he was ready and willing to kill again.'

'I think I agree. Anyway, you've done your part and done it well.'

'Thank you, sir,' said Tansey. He himself felt satisfied with his handling of the case, and the Chief Constable was not in the habit of handing out a compliment. When he got home, Tansey thought, he would be able to boast about it to Hilary, his wife.